FORSAKEN

FORSAKEN

Patricia Robins

CHIVERS

| British Library Cataloguing in Publication Data available |

This Large Print edition published by AudioGO Ltd, Bath, 2012.
Published by arrangement with the Author

U.K. Hardcover   ISBN   978 1 4458 3046 9
U.K. Softcover   ISBN   978 1 4458 3048 3

Printed and bound in Great Britain by
MPG Books Group Limited

CHAPTER ONE

He does love me . . . he does love me! she thought triumphantly as she lay relaxed and near to sleep in the shelter of his arm. He could not have made love so perfectly if he didn't care.

As if by way of denial of her thoughts, he turned suddenly and completely so that now his back was towards her, and a moment later she heard his deep, steady breathing and knew he was asleep.

The pleasant, reassuring glow that had enveloped her as an aftermath of their love-making, left her now to be replaced by a deep-rooted depression. All the old doubts came back to torment her. She lay on her back staring into the darkness of the room from grey-blue eyes that were misted with tears.

There is always one who cares more than the other, she told herself fiercely, determined not to let the tears fall. I must not expect too much of him . . . men are different . . . and he does care . . . he must . . .

Oh, yes, she told herself, suddenly ruthless. He had always cared about the physical side of their marriage. That had been of paramount importance from the first moment of their meeting . . . six years ago? How quickly the time went by and yet in another sense, it

1

seemed a century since those wonderful, ecstatic days of their engagement. Jerry had been thirty-two, she herself twenty-five. Now she would soon be thirty-two and was the mother of two wonderful children. Had the years changed her? A moment or two ago, Jerry had whispered huskily in her ear:

'You're more beautiful than ever, Lynn. You're made for love!'

Other people had told her marriage had improved her looks, her figure, though she knew without vanity that there had never been much wrong with them. But she had lost a little weight and it suited her. She had changed physically, but in herself, not at all. She still loved him as deeply, as desperately, as ever.

'You've changed, Lindy dear!'

That was her aunt . . . her far too observant aunt.

'What makes you so cynical these days? Why are you so bitter, Lindy? You've changed, my dear. Is it Jerry?'

She dreaded those questions . . . dreaded most of all that her aunt might detect that false brightness of her voice when she lied:

'Jerry? Oh, Aunt Meg, you've got a bee in your bonnet about Jerry. We're perfectly happy and he's a wonderful husband.'

Once she had thought her aunt narrow-minded and bigoted because she had raised objections to her marriage when she learned that Jerry was a divorcé.

2

'Not because I'm against divorce in itself, Lindy, although I do believe that if people vow to take each other for better or for worse, they should be willing to take the bad along with the good. But I'm always suspicious when a *woman* divorces her husband. Marriage means so much more to a woman and I don't think wives give up their husbands easily . . . not even these days. *Why* did Jerry's wife divorce him? He's charming, has more than his share of good looks, and money, too. Why should she drag him and herself through the divorce court? Find out that before you marry him, Lindy.'

She had argued hotly in his defence. Jerry's wife had been a bitch . . . there was no other word for her. She had been selfish, self-centred, and had only married him because of his money. She had never really loved him or wanted to make him happy, and had grabbed at the first excuse that had come her way to get rid of him. They'd had a quarrel and he had rushed out of the house and stupidly, no doubt, had got drunk. Then he'd taken a girl back to her flat and passed out and had stayed the night there sleeping it off on the settee. There was no one else there so of course everyone thought the worst, including the porter of the block of flats who supplied the necessary evidence. Jerry hadn't bothered to defend the case, partly to avoid publicity for the girl's sake and partly because he was so fed

3

up with his marriage that he thought it better to let his wife go.

Her aunt had listened to this story without expression. Now she said:

'Jerry told you that himself?'

'Of course! He confessed everything . . . although there wasn't really anything to confess. But he wanted me to hear the truth.'

'He may have wanted you to hear his version of the truth before anyone else told you his wife's version!'

'That's a horrible thing to say, Aunt. What have you got against Jerry? You know I'm in love with him. I'm going to marry him. So why try to find fault? I don't understand you, Aunt Meg.'

'It's only that your happiness means a lot to me, Lynn. I'd rather have you unhappy now than for you to marry the wrong man and be miserable for the rest of your life.'

'He's not the wrong man. We have everything in common. And he's as passionately in love with me as I am with him. Why don't you trust him? Anyone would think you know something about him to his discredit.'

Her aunt had sighed.

'No, I don't know anything against him, Lynn, but my instinct forbids me to trust him. He's too good-looking, too charming, too good to be true, in fact! Forgive me, darling, if what I've been saying hurts you. Believe me,

4

it's only from my desire to protect you. You've always been very dependent on other people emotionally. If your marriage went wrong . . . then you'd have so few weapons with which to defend yourself. You're very vulnerable, my dear . . . as is every passionate and emotional woman once she has fallen in love. But if you're quite sure you're doing the right thing . . . then I'll try to believe in him. Perhaps I am misjudging him.'

No! Lynn thought bitterly. Her aunt's instinct had not been entirely wrong. What would her aunt say now if she knew what kind of husband Jerry had turned out to be? The imagined expression of outrage on her face almost brought a smile to her own.

For the first year, everything had been perfect. Life had been one long honeymoon. Jerry was the perfect lover. He knew exactly the right thing to say and do . . . always. When she was tired, he petted and spoiled her; when she was happy, he outrivalled her gaiety. When she wanted nothing better than a quiet evening alone with him, he would lie on the sofa, running his hands through the gold silk of her hair, talking, drinking, smoking and always, before long, making passionate love to her. In such moods he was utterly irresistible, and if she had loved him before she married him, those first twelve months with him had ensnared her heart and soul for ever. When the second year brought its first disillusionments, she was too deeply entangled to be able to escape.

The second year! It had brought her the greatest joy of her life and the greatest unhappiness. It had brought her David . . . her firstborn, darling son. And it had brought her Jerry's first act of unfaithfulness.

She forgave him. Deeply hurt as she had been, she could understand in a way how it had happened. Jerry, filled with remorse, had explained everything.

'It had nothing to do with *us*, Lynn. Try to understand, my dearest. I didn't love her . . . not for a moment. It was purely physical. You know how close you and I had always been. Then with the baby making you so uncomfortable and you sleeping so badly . . . well, naturally I didn't want to bother you . . . but a man has certain needs, and then when you went off to hospital, Trish just happened to ring up and ask me round for a drink and . . . well, that was that. It was only once, darling, and I felt desperately ashamed afterwards. I'd give the world to be able to undo it. I've not seen her since and in fact I never want to see her again. Say you do understand, Lynn? I couldn't bear anything to come between us *now*.'

Now . . . because he had the little son he had always wanted and they had so often talked about . . . because she had only been back from the hospital a month and it ought to be one of

6

the milestones of happiness in their married life. No, she couldn't bear it either!

'But Jerry, it was the night before David was born . . .'

Did that make it any worse . . . any better? Did it alter the fact that Jerry had been unfaithful to her . . . had held another woman in his arms and made love to her at a time when she was carrying his child . . . perhaps even at the moment she gave birth to him?

'Lynn, forgive me, darling . . . I love you so much . . . forgive me!'

She had forgiven, in so far as it had been possible to forgive. Simply to take him back in her arms, to enfold him again with her love and to behave as if 'it' had never happened . . . that she could do. But the scar that was left on her heart had never completely healed . . . only been buried beneath her determination to forget.

Just over a year later, Sue arrived. Against her will, Lynn found herself watching Jerry closely all through her pregnancy. If he showed signs of restlessness, she forced herself to go out somewhere with him . . . even although she was longing desperately for her bed and sleep. She dreaded the time when she must go into hospital and leave him alone. She didn't . . . couldn't trust him after last time. But perhaps because of the late nights and the worry, Sue started to arrive a month before she was due and with little or no warning. She was born prematurely at home and Lynn had been too ill for a day or two to care any more where Jerry was or be glad that she had not after all had to leave him.

The week after Sue's birth, Jerry had come home drunk. She heard his voice, arguing with the nurse to let him into her room.

'Mrs Birch is sleeping, sir. She needs all the rest she can get. I'm sorry, sir, doctor's orders.'

'To hell with the doctor. She's my wife and I'll see her if I damn well please!'

Wide awake now, she realized that he was very drunk. Every nerve taut, she felt the thud of his body on the hall floor through her own nervous system, causing her to feel so ill that she thought she would indeed be sick. She lay back on the pillows and fought her nausea while, outside the door, she heard her husband giving way to his. She thought of going to him but then she heard the nurse's brisk footsteps and the clink of pail and water, and presently, Jerry's voice again and his unsteady footsteps as he was helped along the passage to his room.

She was desperately ashamed, and when she heard the bedroom door open, she closed her eyes quickly, afraid of what the nurse might say.

'Awake yet, Mrs. Birch? Time to feed Baby. What a pretty little darling she is! I never knew a premature baby so perfect. They are usually crumpled and red! Aren't we lucky, Mrs.

Birch!'

So there was to be no mention of what had just happened outside her door? Did the starched, efficient nurse really believe she had heard nothing?

She looked into the minute, perfectly formed face of her baby and the tiny eyelids opened. Two violet-blue eyes, exact replicas of hers, stared up at her.

Tears suddenly poured down her cheeks. Tears for what? For whom? Not for Jerry! Perhaps they were for herself?

'Come now, Mrs. Birch . . . we mustn't give way to tears. I know it's very easy to cry in your condition, but it isn't good for you or for Baby. Besides, everything is quite all right. Doctor says Baby is as strong as a full-term baby and believe me, Mrs. Birch, he'd soon have had her into hospital if she'd been the slightest bit at risk.'

Her tears had dried . . . but so had her milk. Of the abundance she'd had to offer David, there was now none for Sue. None the less, Sue had thrived, and as Nurse had said . . . she was strong and healthy. Everything was all right.

'Oh, Jerry, how could you? If you had to get drunk, at least you didn't have to come home.'

'Good God, Lynn, is there no satisfying you? You worried yourself sick if I was out of sight for five minutes. Don't think I didn't see you watching me with an eagle eye in case I

9

repeated the Trish affair. Now you're grousing because I did come home!'

It had been several weeks before she had forgiven him . . . not so much for his weakness but for the hurt he dealt her when he tried to brazen it out. Then, with Sue firmly established on the bottle and her aunt worrying her to death because she looked so ghastly and the doctor urging Jerry to take her for a good long holiday . . . she agreed to let her aunt take Sue and David for a month while she went away alone with Jerry.

Another honeymoon. Truculent though she had been at the start, Jerry had worn down her defences. He was utterly considerate, tender, adoring, and had endless patience with her bouts of weeping. Within a week, she was almost her old self again, and by the end of the holiday they were perfectly reunited. Her new-found happiness had brought back the light to her eyes, the shine to her hair, the smile to her lips. She had put back the weight she had lost after Sue's birth and as Jerry told her as he held her to him: 'You're more alluring than ever, Lynn darling. God, how I love you! There's something about you . . . something I can't explain. It gets me every time. I could never live without you, Lynn.'

She settled down to making a happy home for Jerry and the babies. David and Sue thrived and she loved them utterly, but with a different love from the helpless

10

surrender of her being to Jerry. Her love for the children was fierce and protective and carefully controlled. She never gave them too much . . . only sufficient for their needs. They were beautiful, contented, attractive toddlers. Jerry, a little impatient sometimes with other children, never seemed bored by his own. David was her image . . . Sue, whose eyes had lost their blueness and had become as dark as Jerry's own, was in almost every way his physical double. She had his rather large, full mouth and the same way of lifting the corner of her upper lip when she smiled. Her hair was as dark and curled across her head just as Jerry's did when he had bathed or been swimming. She was a beautiful child . . . slightly Spanish looking with her warm, dark colouring and bright personality. Jerry's child. She, Lynn, felt a special love for this image of the man she had married and who was, even after four years of matrimony, as wildly attractive to her as ever. Yet deep in her heart, she watched and studied Sue . . . waiting for any signs of that other side of Jerry which could be so selfish, so ruthless, so destructive in its egotism and vanity. One of the reasons Jerry so adored Sue was that he saw himself in her so clearly.

David was like herself . . . tall, slender, supple, fair. His hair was straight and boyish and his blue eyes intelligent, thoughtful, breaking sometimes into a quick, delightful

11

smile as he saw the humour in a situation. At three, he took the most painstaking care of Sue and was constantly hurt by her baby independence. He wanted so much to be needed and yet Sue so seldom seemed to need his help! He was sensitive and at times critical . . . yet once he gave his love or friendship, it was never withdrawn or lessened. At five he still gave 'Mr. Milkman' (his hero at three) his quick, welcoming smile. He, too, adored his father, but Lynn always felt that while he was scrupulously fair in handing out affection to both his parents, it was to her that he gave most of his real self.

At six, David took a sudden, deep-rooted aversion to his father. Lynn closed her eyes as she recalled the painful memory of David's birthday . . . only a month ago now. She had planned a children's party for him on a Saturday afternoon . . . because then Jerry would be at home and it meant so much more to the children if Daddy was there. He made everything such fun and children always loved him. 'The perfect father', her friends and even her aunt had had to admit!

Jerry had phoned her from the office at lunch time when he should have been home.

'Frightfully sorry, darling, but there was an important board meeting this morning and now one of the directors wants me to lunch with him . . . don't see that I can get out of it. But I'll be back by tea time if not before. Tell

12

David I've got a surprise for the party!'

She hadn't worried . . . not until four o'clock. David and Sue had asked several times if he wasn't coming after all and she had reassured them that he would be back before tea. Now the children were getting a little restless and she knew it was time to suggest another game or tea. Should she wait for Jerry? She gave him another fifteen minutes and then let the children start on the party fare.

'We won't light the candles till Daddy comes, will we, Mummy?

'No, darling, we'll wait. He's sure to be here soon.'

Tea was soon consumed and the children's little guests waited expectantly for the cake. Lynn consulted David in a whisper.

'I think perhaps we shouldn't wait for Daddy any longer, darling. If we blow the candles out quickly, then we can light them later when he arrives so that he can see them.'

'But the cake will be all eaten!' David said anxiously. 'It'll be spoilt!'

What was Jerry doing? He was the one who had established the birthday ritual—who, when she brought in the cake declared that it was far too nice to eat.

'Mummy shall put it in a glass case and we'll keep it to look at till next birthday.' . . . Howls of objection from the children. 'Well, perhaps we'll cut just a tiny, tiny bit to taste. Um . . .

yes, it's great! Much too nice to eat! Into the glass case with it, Mummy . . . the kids don't want to eat it!'

How wonderful it tasted when at last it was on the children's plates. How they loved being tempted and teased, knowing all the time that they would have it in the end.

Jerry, this is the first time you've missed one of their birthday parties! Not even a director is excuse enough. Please come back now . . . quickly.

He came at bedtime. The last of the visiting children had gone and David and Sue were tired and a little over-excited by the party. As she bathed them they kept asking why Daddy hadn't come and, tired herself, she had begun to be furiously angry with Jerry. It wasn't the first time he had been late back on a Saturday . . . but never on a birthday. He *knew* how much it meant to the children.

'There he is! I hearded the key!' Sue shouted, hopping up and down and leaving a trail of wet footprints on the bathroom floor.

'Daddy . . . Dad-dee!'

He came upstairs and opened the bathroom door. His face was flushed and he seemed not the slightest bit contrite.

'Sorry to have missed the party, poppets!' he said gaily. 'You know I'd have come if I could.'

Sue threw herself into his arms and chattered excitedly about the balloons, the cake, the party games. David sat in the bath,

14

his eyes unsmiling, as they studied his father's face.

'But *why* didn't you come, Daddy?'

'Yes, *why*?' asked Lynn, knowing just how hurt David was . . . how he was feeling.

She helped him out of the bath and wrapped him in the bath towel, then nodded her head to Jerry. At least it would be some consolation if Daddy dried him and dressed him in his pyjamas. It was always looked on as a treat. She had started to pull Sue's pyjama top over her head when she heard David say:

'Put me down, Daddy! You smell nasty. Put me down!'

'Well, of all the cheek . . .' Jerry began, when he met Lynn's eyes and his own dropped suddenly. 'Dash it all, I had to have the drinks I was offered, Lynn. You know what these directors are. I couldn't look a complete idiot and say "Sorry, old chap, my wife won't let me!"'

The tone of his voice was angry, sarcastic. She felt her own temper rising but controlled it. Whatever happened, she would not let the children know what she was feeling, thinking.

'You still haven't said why you didn't come to my party!' David broke in persistently.

'And I'm damned if I will say why now after that remark of yours, young man!'

A moment later the door slammed behind him and Sue said:

'Look, Mummy, David's crying. Has he
15

hurted himself?'

I'll never forgive him for that. I hate him! Lynn thought savagely as she comforted David and hurried Sue off to bed. But later, she *did* forgive him.

'Do you think I didn't *want* to come to the party, Lynn? You know very well nothing would have made me miss such an occasion if it hadn't been vital. As a matter of fact, I think this afternoon's work is going to get me promoted. Henderson as good as told me that he was going to see that I got a step up before Christmas. You don't understand how these things work, darling. It's not just a matter of whether you're good at the job or not. Personal feelings come into it too . . . and not a little, either. If the higher-ups *like* you, then they take a personal interest in you. I was looking forward to getting home to tell you the good news and all I get is a mountain of abuse from you and David. It might have been of interest to him to know that if I do get this rise, I intend to take you all for a ski-ing holiday this Christmas. You know how David has been badgering us to go to Switzerland ever since he saw that film on ski-ing.'

'Oh, Jerry, do you really think we might go? David will be thrilled to death, I know. Go and tell him, darling. I do so hate to see him in tears on his birthday. But he wasn't being cheeky . . . just telling the truth. A lot of children don't like the smell of whisky . . .

16

as a matter of fact I don't myself . . . and he's only just six, you know. You can't expect him to hide his feelings . . . to be tactful.'

'All right, all right, don't keep on about the whisky. I only had three, you know. I'm not tight!'

If she wasn't careful she would become a nagging wife, Lynn thought, and it would be her fault if Jerry did end up an alcoholic!

'Jerry, darling, I'm not criticizing. It was just that the children were so disappointed and I didn't understand how particularly important this afternoon was. After all, Saturday isn't usually a business day, is it? Congratulations on the rise.'

He put his arm round her and drew her close.

'Well, it hasn't happened yet, you know. Still, it's as good as in the bag. And it'll mean quite a bit to you, too, Lynn. That's one of the reasons I'm so pleased. You'll be able to have lots of new clothes and we could probably afford an *au pair* too.'

'No, you know I don't want that!' Lynn had said. 'I love looking after the house and children myself. Come on, darling, let's go and tell David the good news. He'll be thrilled.'

'Wow, ski-ing!' David had said. 'That'ud be smashing, Daddy. When will we go? Will we really come down a mountain like that man did? As fast as he was going? Is it easy? What a smashing surprise.'

17

But it was Lynn's hand he clutched and later, as she turned out the light, he said:

'Mummy, it was a really good party but I do wish Daddy'd been here too. He did *promise* to come in time.'

David hadn't been able to forgive so easily and he had never quite trusted Jerry's promises since. Only now, remembering, did Lynn realize that when Jerry promised something, David always said: 'Word of honour, Daddy? Cross your heart and cut your throat?'

Lynn shut her eyes, trying to recapture the languor and fatigue of a few minutes past. She turned slightly and with her lips, touched the back of Jerry's head. A wave of tenderness swept over her . . . of remembered passion. Dear, dear Jerry. Of course he had his faults. Everyone had. No one was perfect; and most of the while, Jerry *was* perfect . . . as a husband and a father. Aunt Meg was wrong to say he was 'too good to be true'. He had been unfaithful to her . . . but only once. He had got a bit tight once in a while but so, probably, did most men. And every marriage had its bad patches. People couldn't be loving and affectionate all the time. If Jerry was occasionally rude and aggressive and said things which hurt . . . well, they did hurt, but it wasn't as if he really meant them. He did love her . . . in his way . . . as much as she loved him in her way.

'It's just that I've always loved him a little bit more than he loves me!' she told herself, sleepy now and content with her lot. There's always one who cares more and I dare say it's usually the woman.

Two minutes later, she was asleep.

CHAPTER TWO

'Lynn, darling, can you get a baby-sitter for tonight and come to a small party we're giving on the spur of the moment?'

Lynn disentangled Sue's fingers, chocolate-covered from her interrupted lunch, and shifted the telephone to her other hand.

'We'd love to, Marion! At least, I would, and Jerry always enjoys your parties. We're not doing anything, but it's just possible Jerry may be kept late in town. He's up to his eyes these days and it's sometimes ten before he gets home. Shall I ring you back after I've phoned him?'

Marion's good-natured voice came back promptly.

'It won't matter if Jerry can't manage it till later. In fact, if that does happen, then come to dinner. Jack's brother has just arrived home from Singapore . . . I don't think you've met him, darling, but he's a poppet! So the party is to be a welcome home for him and

19

to introduce him to some people. He's been abroad for five years and doesn't know a soul in England. If you come alone it will make a foursome for dinner and the real crowd will be coming in about half-nineish.'

'Then I'll ring Jerry and let you know definitely!' Lynn said. 'I must fly now, Marion . . . middle of Sue's lunch!'

With Sue packed off for her usual afternoon rest, Lynn took the first opportunity of telephoning Jerry's office. She very seldom did this for he had often told her he hated being rung at work unless it was urgent. His voice always sounded very cold and unfriendly when she did ring and now she never did so unless it was absolutely necessary.

He had not yet gone out for lunch.

'You just caught me, Lynn. Everyone else has gone. What's up?'

Lynn explained and heard Jerry's small sigh of regret.

'It's a bit of a bore, sweetheart, but I can't help it . . . I can tell you now I'm fairly certain to be late. Still, if you're able to make up a foursome for dinner, maybe it's for the best. I'll try to be there by nine.'

'What about a meal for you?' Lynn asked, disappointed in spite of herself, and worried for Jerry, too. He seemed to get longer and longer hours of work as he rose up the ladder. Of course, she could understand that extra responsibility meant extra work but he looked

20

so frightfully tired after those late evenings at the office.

'Don't worry about me, darling. How's things?'

'Everything's fine!' Lynn said. 'Sue's resting and David's at school of course. Jerry, do get a decent lunch if you're going to miss dinner. You know Marion's parties. You'll need something inside you.'

'Don't fuss, sweetheart. As a matter of fact, I'm lunching with Henderson. I think his niece will be there, too, and it's a slap-up do at the Dorchester. That's why I'll have to catch up on some urgent work this evening. I expect it will be pretty dull but I couldn't very well refuse and anyway, it will be a decent meal. Wish you could be there, too.'

Lynn quickly quenched the little stab of jealousy that assailed her . . . and envy, too. Jerry seemed to lead such an interesting life even if it was all tied up with his work. She said lightly:

'No flirting with the beautiful niece, darling! Remember you're a married man!'

'As if I could forget when I've got the most glamorous wife in the world. Anyway, as she's related to Henderson, she's probably as ugly as sin. Well, see you later, darling. About nineish.'

Marion Castle was a very old and much loved friend of Lynn's. They'd been at school together and had never allowed their later

21

individual paths to separate them. They had corresponded regularly and often arranged their holidays to coincide. An only child, Marion had been to Lynn like a twin sister and there was little or nothing they did not know about each other.

Marion, Lynn thought as the taxi drove her through the streets to her party, was the only person in the world who knew *all* the facts of her life with Jerry. She alone had been told of Jerry's one act of unfaithfulness and his two lapses with the bottle. Marion had always liked Jerry and yet sometimes Lynn had wondered if her friend was not a little too uncritical of Jerry when they had discussed him before her engagement. It seemed odd that Marion should be so approving at the same time as her aunt was so oddly suspicious of the man she had chosen to marry.

'He's just the type of husband you need, darling!' Marion had told her. 'You're too introspective, too serious, old dear. Jerry will help you to accept things that happen as a matter of course. He's such fun to be with, isn't he? And so wildly attractive. If I hadn't already lost my poor heart to Jack, I'd have made a play for him myself. Not that he would have looked at me! He likes glamour and you've got it, Lynn. I've always been a plain Jane and really and truly, I don't care so long as Jack thinks I'm tops. At least I know he loves me for myself! No, darling, you'll make a perfect pair . . . complement each other. Congratulations, Lynn.'

When told about Jerry's unfaithfulness, Marion had been slightly sobered in her opinion but had glossed over it in a way that had never occurred to Lynn who was desperately shaken and upset.

'After all, darling, you must look at it from Jerry's point of view. First, he's a man and I've always been led to understand that men can have an affair with a woman they don't necessarily care twopence about. The physical side is quite a thing apart from the love angle. Secondly, he is frightfully attractive and he must be subjected to a lot more temptation than, say, Jack. I dare say this Trish female set her cap at him and more or less seduced him. It probably wasn't Jerry's fault really . . . a few drinks too many and he just didn't know what he was doing.'

'But I couldn't have been unfaithful to Jerry, Marion. Even making allowances for the fact that Jerry's male and it may not have meant much to him, he must have known how much it would hurt me. I wouldn't do anything ever to hurt him . . . to risk losing his respect for me . . . perhaps even to risk losing him altogether.'

'Well, I don't suppose he expected to be found out!' Marion said practically. 'You're too old-fashioned, Lynn. I'm not saying I don't agree with your ideals . . . as a matter of fact, I do. But you have to make allowances for men

23

like Jerry. You're not going to let it ruin your marriage, surely? After all, you've admitted often that your relationship was near perfect. To carve it up because of a woman who means nothing at all to Jerry seems madness . . . specially now you've got David, too.'

'I know, Marion. But Jerry has done more than hurt my pride. Something closed up inside me and won't get warm again. I don't want Jerry to touch me now. I can't just write it off the way he seems able to do. It's changed my feelings for him. I can't respect him now.'

But in the end, she had forgiven and she and Jerry had become lovers again. As usual, it was as satisfying and complete a union as it had ever been. She had not really stopped loving him and Marion knew it.

Dear Marion! and dear Jack, too. They were both so plain and frumpy and yet so good-natured and amusing! They had masses of friends of all kinds! No one could help liking them. It was a shame they had no children of their own. It was the one wrong note in the marriage.

I suppose there is always something to prevent the absolutely perfect marriage! Lynn thought, sighing for her lost illusions. If you look into the lives of any two people, there is always a flaw somewhere.

Jack's brother, Philip, was not unlike him to look at and just as charming. Lynn liked him from the start. He was not in the least attractive to her physically—his features, colouring, stature being as nondescript as Jack's, but the whole was pleasing in a big, St. Bernardish kind of way. He was tall, square and rather vague in his manner and untidy in appearance. But when he spoke, his voice was deep and attractive and his smile was shy and boyish. He was older than Jack . . . thirty-eight, Marion had told her. Lynn could well believe that underneath that shy, vague surface lay concealed real depths of character.

Philip's job had taken him back to Singapore for the last five years but at last he had been sent home to England . . . with mixed feelings about his homecoming, he confided to Lynn.

'Fact is, I got used to living in the Far East. I don't make friends very easily, and I must confess I'm a bit scared at the prospect of beginning all over again.'

'Why have you come home?' Lynn asked, interested quite a little in this large, ungainly man.

'My boss thought it time I widened my interests!' he told her, with his sudden, shy smile. 'I'm at Head Office now and have got to find myself a flat in town. I believe from all Marion tells me it isn't easy these days.'

'I think it's less difficult for a bachelor!' Lynn consoled him, laughing. 'Landlords always approve of bachelors. You're not married, are you?'

'No, I'd like to be, though. Just not yet met the right girl. Now I'm probably too old and set in my ways to make a good husband.'

'Rubbish!' said Jack, as he came across the room with two coffee cups. 'Just the right time to settle down now you've sown your wild oats. Trouble with Pip, Lynn, is that he's far too particular. Always was. I can remember, when we were at Oxford, chasing any pretty girl I could find, but Pip would stick his ugly great nose in the air and push off somewhere with a boat or a fishing rod.'

'You make me sound a misogynist!' his brother said, that smile again transforming his face from the ugly into the attractive. 'It was merely that I found all those pretty girls of yours rather vacuous and . . . well . . . lacking in depth, I suppose.'

'You can't afford to be too fussy, old man!' Jack said, laughing. 'Not with your ugly old pate. Nor me, either. Look what I've had to make do with.'

But the look he cast his wife was full of love and adoration and Marion, who had joined them, laughed unconcernedly.

'I'm the perfect wife, Pip. And there's plenty more like me. You don't want a glamour girl like Lynn . . . the flighty kind! Choose a nice, plump, homely girl like your sister-in-law.'

'That's not fair!' Lynn objected, smiling. 'I'm neither glamorous nor flighty. And I'm just as home-loving as you are.'

26

'All right, darling, I'll give in about the flighty part and the homey part, but you remain a little piece of glamour. Don't you agree, Pip?'

'I think she is one of the most beautiful women I've ever met,' Philip said quietly.

'You're a hit with the world's prize misogynist!' Jack said, slapping Pip on the back. 'Congratulations, Lynn. Still, she's got a husband already, old boy. Too late, too late!'

'Jack, stop fooling and go and answer the bell. Our first guests are arriving. Will Jerry be here soon, Lynn? It's almost nine.'

The room filled rapidly with people and drinks were circulated. Lynn chattered to the people she knew and watched the door for Jerry. Much as she enjoyed an occasional party, she could never really settle down to having a good time unless Jerry was there with her. She began as always to worry about him if he were later than half an hour or so after the time he had told her he would arrive. It was silly . . . but somehow she couldn't help it. He was the only man in the world she really gave a hoot about and if anything happened to him . . . an accident . . .

'Can I get you another drink, Lynn? I don't think I know your other name. Marion and Jack have always called you just Lynn in their letters.'

'That's good enough for me!' Lynn said,

turning to Philip who was at her elbow. 'I don't think I do want a drink, thanks awfully. What I really would like is a chair. Sue—that's my little daughter, Marion's god-child—walked me off my feet this afternoon and I'm suddenly rather tired.'

Within a few moments, he had found a seat for her and brought her a large cup of coffee. She hadn't realized how much she'd wanted it until then.

She looked more closely at the man beside her and thought how out of place he seemed amongst these other people. He was wearing slacks, and a blazer over a polo-necked sweater; and was smoking a pipe. Nearly every other man in the room was in a dark lounge suit.

He turned suddenly and caught her eye.

'I'm sorry now I didn't change. Fact is, I've been feeling the cold a bit since I got home. Jack said it didn't matter what I wore but I see now I've done the wrong thing.'

Lynn was instantly sympathetic.

'I wasn't criticizing you!' she said, suddenly shy herself. 'As a matter of fact I prefer men in casual clothes and I wish I could persuade Jerry to smoke a pipe. I love the smell. But he won't give up his cigarettes. Philip . . . did you find me this chair by the door . . . on purpose?'

He gave her a quick look and then glanced away again.

'Well, I just thought you might want to be

28

somewhere where you could see your husband when he arrived.'

'Thank you!' she said. 'That was thoughtful. I suppose I'm absurdly old-fashioned . . . I mean, most wives at a party probably don't mind whether their husbands are there or not. But . . . well, I . . . I suppose I'm just silly about mine.'

'It's not silly to be in love!'

She bit her lip thoughtfully. What a strange conversation this was turning out to be . . . in the middle of a noisy, laughing crowd, too.

'I've been married six years!' she said, her tone self-derogatory. 'I ought to be over that "can't bear him out of my sight" stage!'

'I think it's wonderfully refreshing to find a woman who still feels that way in spite of six years of marriage.'

'Now you're being cynical.'

'I didn't mean to be. It's just that people seem to have become so . . . so fickle nowadays. You notice it more and more. You say you're old-fashioned. Maybe I am, too, come to that. But it seems to me to be natural to want to be with the people you love. You're not worrying about your husband . . . I mean, is he very late?'

Lynn glanced at her watch.

'Well, it's after ten and Jerry said nine. But I expect he'll be here soon.'

'Oh, Lord!' Philip said suddenly. 'There are some people I know. I ought to go and be polite.'

'But of course!' Lynn said quickly. 'I'll go and see if I can give Marion a hand with the drinks or something.'

She felt his hand, suddenly, on her arm.

'No, don't go. I'd far rather stay here and talk to you. It's all right as long as they don't notice me. I can talk to them later . . . when your husband comes.'

Lynn felt flattered in spite of herself. How simple and direct this man was, in spite of his shyness. He made it quite clear that he enjoyed her company.

'You said you had no friends in England,' she reminded him for something to say.

'Well, these aren't really friends . . . some English acquaintances I met in Singapore. The husband and I did business together. It's that couple over there . . . the woman in that red thing!'

Lynn followed his directions and saw immediately the woman he was speaking about. She was a tall, slender, dark girl of about her own age . . . and very strikingly beautiful. The 'thing' looked like a Dior model!

'She's very attractive!' she said to Philip. 'Is she nice, too?'

'I thought so. I didn't know them very well . . . at least, not her. They'd only just been married and it was really business and honeymoon combined. Hedges, her husband, worships the ground she treads on and I think she's very fond of him. She'd been married before, you know. Hedges told me about it. She was terribly cut up for a while after the divorce . . . I think she really loved her first husband in spite of all he did to her. Women are funny the way they can love a womanizer.'

'Was he?' Lynn asked curiously.

'Hedges said so. He was always fooling round with other women and he used to hit the bottle, too. In the end she divorced him. I think she was going to have a baby and there was a row or something and she lost it. Soon after that she divorced him. Hedges had known her for years and had always been in love with her but it was three years after that before she married him. As this party was really for me tonight, Jack insisted I ask anyone I knew. Hedges is going out to Singapore again soon, so I thought it would be a good opportunity to have a chat with him about one or two things I left unfinished out there. But I can see him later.'

'This party is in your honour and I ought not to monopolize you like this!' Lynn said. 'Look, why not let me introduce you to some of the people here? I know most of them.'

'No, please don't. I'd rather stay and talk to you. I'm not very good at meeting people . . . always afraid I'll bore them and I usually do, I expect.'

'I haven't been bored,' Lynn said. 'You

shouldn't be so self-deprecatory, if there is such a word! You know, it would do you good to be married . . . draw you out of yourself. I'm going to help Marion and Jack find you a nice girl.'

He turned and smiled at her.

'No, please don't. Why do people always imagine you need a husband or wife to be happy? Women especially are inveterate matchmakers!'

'Perhaps we married couples feel that the matrimonial state is the happiest one,' Lynn smiled back at him.

'It's a refreshing thought . . . but is it true? I know so few happy couples.'

'But that's silly,' Lynn said quickly. 'Look at Jack and Marion!'

'Yes, I grant you them. But how many others?'

'There's me!'

'Are you happy?'

'But yes, of course I am. What made you ask?'

He shrugged his shoulders as if her question had embarrassed him.

'No, really. I want to know. Don't I look happy?'

'Well, if you insist, the answer is "not particularly". But I expect that's because you're worrying . . . about your husband being late, I mean. I'm sure you're very happy . . . I don't know what made me ask such a personal question. Please forgive me.'

'There's nothing to forgive,' Lynn said, anxious to put him at ease. 'After all, it isn't as if we were strangers. Marion and Jack have spoken of you so often I feel you're an old friend.' (Strange how true this was!)

'They often wrote to me about you, too,' Philip said. 'I suppose that's why I felt I knew you so well as soon as you came into the room tonight. I don't think I felt so awkward as I usually do with women. I never know what to say to them as a rule! All the same, my . . . my remark was . . . was—'

'Jerry!'

He broke off as Lynn jumped to her feet and all but ran across the room to greet the man who was coming in. Philip Castle lifted his pipe to his mouth and studied the man who, in the last few hours, had come to have such meaning for him. He wasn't fully aware of the fact yet, but for the first time in his thirty-eight years he had fallen in love. Later, he was to reflect, not without bitterness, that it would have had to be with a woman quite outside his reach. Someone as beautiful as Lynn would never care a jot for a dull old stick-in-the-mud such as himself even if she were not already heart and soul another man's.

Her intense love for her husband had made a mark on his mind and he was now interested to see the man to whom she ran so eagerly. Dispassionately, he appraised the fellow as

33

he stooped to kiss his wife's cheek. Good-looking, almost too handsome; Philip could see how he might be so attractive to Lynn . . . dark hair curling across his forehead in spite of the attempts to brush it flat; dark, interesting eyes with a distinctly challenging look to them; a nicely tanned, well-shaped face. Only his mouth spoiled the general effect of healthy masculine charm. It was a little too full, too sensual; somehow weak. All the same, he, a man, could judge this other man's physical attributes and give him nearly full marks.

Lynn dragged Jerry across to Marion and Jack to apologize for his lateness.

'Couldn't help it, poppet,' he had told her regretfully. 'Ran into a chap I know who'd been trying to contact me about some business . . . well, I won't bore you with the details . . . but I had to give him a drink, which made me miss the eight ten. So sorry, darling.'

'You're here now!' Lynn said happily. 'Come and meet Jack's brother . . . he's awfully nice. I'm going to ask him along to dinner soon. I've been chatting to him most of the evening.'

She looked round the crowded room and saw Philip talking to the girl in the red dress and her husband. She caught Jerry's sleeve and pulled him towards them.

Philip turned as she touched his shoulder.

'Pip, this is Jerry . . . darling, Jack's . . .'
Her voice trailed away uncomfortably as

34

she saw that Jerry was not listening. He was staring at the girl in the red dress, his face grey beneath the tan, his expression . . . well, almost shocked. Then, as she watched him, he seemed to assume a sudden armour of gaiety and, to her, his voice sounded oddly rasping as he said:

'Why, hullo Jane! Long time no see. Let me introduce my wife, Lynn! Lynn, this is Jane!'

Lynn looked at the girl wondering curiously how it was that Jerry knew her and she did not. The girl was very pale but she seemed poised and quite controlled as she said:

'My husband, Robert!'

For a moment, Lynn felt the other woman's dark eyes on her face and then heard her voice, low, husky, saying:

'I've often wondered when we should meet. I . . . I used to know your husband a long time ago, Mrs. Birch. Fancy running into him here.'

'Nice surprise!' she heard Jerry's voice, the enthusiasm somehow forced. 'Do you know Marion and Jack well? I wasn't aware you'd met them.'

'We're friends of Pip's!' Robert Hedges said quietly. 'We only met our host and hostess this evening.'

'I'll get some drinks!' Jerry said moving quickly away.

'I'm afraid we interrupted your conversation,' Lynn apologised, breaking an awkward silence.

35

'As a matter of fact, we were just going, weren't we, Jane?' Robert Hedges said quickly . . . pointedly. The girl nodded and Lynn knew that there had been no such intention till now. Somehow Jerry's arrival had prompted them to leave. *Why?* 'If you'll excuse us . . . Mrs. Birch . . . we'll find Jack and Marion and say our thank-yous. You've got my telephone number, Philip. Give me a ring and we'll lunch next week.'

'Good-bye, Mrs. Birch!'

Lynn felt her hand touched by the girl's cool fingers; met again the glance in those dark, strangely sympathetic eyes, then they were gone.

'Philip!'

'Come and sit down!'

She obeyed him, feeling as if she were in the grip of some peculiar dream in which everyone knew what was going on except herself.

'I . . . I didn't realize your husband knew the Hedges . . . wonder what's happened to those drinks . . . you stay here, Lynn. I'll see if I can track him down and tell him where we're sitting.'

But Jerry came back without him and Lynn knew that Philip had chosen this way to leave them alone while Jerry explained.

'Jerry, who was she? You seemed quite . . . well, surprised to see her.'

'Who? Jane? Oh, just a girl I used to know. Odd running into her again.'

36

His voice was far too casual and she knew him too well to let it pass.

'Jerry, don't . . . don't be so mysterious. Tell me about her. Why did they push off so quickly? Were you in love with her once? Why didn't the husband—'

'Give us a chance, Lynn,' Jerry broke in roughly. 'My God, how boring jealous women can be.'

'Jerry!'

'Well, for Heaven's sake. Surely I can run into an ex-girlfriend without you getting green-eyed. There's nothing to fuss about. It was all over and done with ages ago.'

'I didn't say it wasn't,' Lynn said, torn between anger at his tone of voice and a sudden conviction that he was lying to her. 'I was just curious to know why it should be such a shock to you both. She looked stunned and the husband looked daggers. Anyone would imagine you'd had an affair with her and the husband knew about it. You must admit their attitude wasn't exactly normal.'

'Well, if you must know, that fool Hedges was in love with her at the same time I was and he was always eaten up with jealousy. He got her in the end so I don't see why he need carry on the antagonism.'

'Maybe she . . . she was still in love with you . . . when she married him,' Lynn said quietly, wondering why Jerry was being so violent, so angry. The whole business seemed to grow more puzzling than ever.

'Jerry, was it before . . . before we were married?'

'My God, woman, of course it was!'

In spite of the fact that she knew he was beginning to lose his temper with her, Lynn had to go on.

'Before you . . . your first marriage?'

She felt a slight shock to her nervous system as Jerry looked at her for a long moment from eyes that seemed to be coldly furious . . . as if in that minute he hated her. Then she heard his voice say:

'If you insist on knowing, she was my first wife!'

Then he turned and left her.

Lynn was stunned. When she could think coherently, she found Philip once again in the chair beside her, handing her a drink.

'You look ghastly!' he said. 'Sip this.'

Obediently, she drank a little of the whisky. She was too bowled over to wonder how he had managed to come back at the precise moment she needed him.

'That girl . . . your friend . . . in the red dress . . . she was my husband's first wife!'

'You mean, Jane . . . Mrs. Hedges?'

She nodded, the pieces of the puzzle suddenly falling into place.

She had always known that Jerry's wife was called Janet. Once or twice Jerry had mentioned her as Netta . . . but Jane was another derivative and perhaps she had chosen this in preference to Jerry's old name for her when she married again.

She had never seen a photograph . . . Jerry told her he had destroyed them all because he had ceased to care what became of her and certainly didn't want any reminder of her around the place. Funny, she could even recall those very words. She had known, too, that Janet had reverted to her maiden name, Crawley. When Philip had spoken of Jane Hedges, there was no possible means of recognition.

So after all these years, she had met her predecessor . . . thought her astonishingly beautiful . . . and not the least like the woman of her imagination. This girl had not looked hard . . . sophisticated, perhaps, smart; but never could that soft full mouth be described as cruel, nor the liquid brown eyes anything but sensitive. Somehow Jerry's description of his first wife and her own impressions of Jane Hedges would not . . . could not be reconciled.

'I just don't understand.' She said the words aloud. Then as she lifted her face appealingly to Philip, she suddenly remembered, just as he was doing, those remarks he had made only a short while earlier.

'She loved him in spite of all he did to her . . . a thoroughly bad lot . . . fooling around with other women . . . hit the bottle . . .'

Her eyes widened and a deep red suffused

her cheeks as she stared helplessly at the embarrassed man beside her.

'There's been some mistake!' she said violently. 'There must be some mistake . . .'

But all Philip could find to say was, 'Sorry . . . I'm so sorry!' as his fingers twirled the unlit pipe round and round in his large, sensitive hands.

CHAPTER THREE

They had driven home in comparative silence. Once or twice Jerry whistled tunelessly or made some comment on the evening; but no mention was made, as yet, of the episode which had so upset Lynn.

They were in bed and Jerry was smoking a last cigarette when Lynn could bear the strained atmosphere between them no longer.

'Darling!'

His eyes remained fixed on the end of his cigarette. She noticed how square and practical his hands looked and remembered inconsequently what power they could exercise on her body.

'Uh-huh?'

Was he going to behave as if nothing extraordinary had happened? He could not be so insensitive to her feelings! He was going to brazen it out, she supposed and then corrected herself. Jerry was in no way to blame. There had been nothing to blame him for. He had not known how Philip . . . and probably other people . . . described Jane Hedges' first husband. She had no right to believe those things which could be no more than hearsay . . . gossip. Six years ago, she would not even have listened, but now . . . now she could not be untouched by suspicion. The description so aptly fitted Jerry . . . her own experience of Jerry. No, that wasn't fair. He had been no more unfaithful than hundreds of other husbands . . . just unfortunately discovered; he had been no more drunk than probably thousands of husbands and each time there had been extenuating circumstances.

'Jerry, please talk to me . . . about her. You've never done so. I don't altogether understand.'

Her voice pleaded with him. She did not want a scene, a row, with Jerry losing his temper and flinging things round the room; perhaps even waking the children. It not only hurt her, but frightened her that in those violent moods he could be so different from the Jerry she loved . . . *the real Jerry.*

'I don't see what there is to talk about. What don't you understand?'

His tone of voice was merely surprised.

Her fingers played with the fold of the top sheet. She did not look at him.

'Well, perhaps it's that she . . . Jane . . .

Janet . . . did not quite seem to fit your description of her. I always believed her very hard-boiled, to use your own word, a bitch. She didn't strike me that way at all.'

He turned then and looked at her with an expression she could not read.

'My dear girl, you only met her for a few minutes, and if I remember rightly, you barely said two words to each other. How can you possibly know what she's really like? Plenty of women *look* soft and gentle and sweet and are hard as nails underneath.'

She felt relief flooding through her. After all, what Jerry had just said was absolutely true. One's impression of a person could so easily be wrong. Only her instinct had drawn her to the girl in the red dress. Something about the soft, sad, luminous dark eyes had struck an answering chord in herself. But that could have been nothing more than the outcome of Philip's influence. He had spoken nicely of her . . . caused her, Lynn, to feel sympathetic towards her before they had even met. Philip . . . there lay the real trouble . . . it was what Philip had said about the man Jane used to be married to . . . about Jerry!

'Someone at the party told me a bit about her; said she had a pretty raw deal from her first husband. They gave me the impression she was the injured party in the divorce.'

'Well, for God's sake!' Jerry said irritably. 'Do you prefer to take some stranger's word to mine? Have I ever lied to you? Who said so, anyway? That fellow Castle you were mooching round with most of the evening, I suppose.'

Lynn had been anxious to keep Philip out of the discussion but since she had barely spoken to anyone else, and in any case few other people there, if any, could have known Jane Hedges, there seemed no object in denying Philip as the origin of the remark.

'It just seems so odd . . . two such opposite points of view,' she said uneasily.

'Naturally there are two opposite points of view. Her friends took her side . . . mine took my side. That's obvious, isn't it?'

'Darling, please don't shout at me. I can hear you well enough and you'll wake Sue. Yes, I suppose it is obvious. It's only that I never knew till now that there were two points of view. I mean, I always imagined that the marriage had been hopeless because she wasn't prepared to put anything into it; that she didn't really love you at all.'

'Love!' The word came out almost scornfully. 'How in Heaven's name can any man put a name to women's emotions? She was attracted to me, but that didn't mean she loved me.'

'But Philip said she did!'

He turned on her, suddenly furious.

'The blasted fool! Take his word if you want to but in Heaven's name stop ramming his theories down my throat at this time of night. I'm sick and tired of the discussion.'

He turned round and switched off the bedside lamp, plunging the room into darkness just as his voice had plunged her heart into an aching void.

'Jerry . . . please don't let's quarrel! There's no earthly need to be rude to me over a . . . discussion. Please, darling . . .'

I'm afraid . . . she thought . . . afraid always to let a quarrel take its full course. I'm afraid in case he'll stop loving me; start hating me. I'd rather bear anything than that. I'm afraid . . . and I have no pride.

'Jerry!'

He turned suddenly and a moment later his arms were round her, holding her so tightly that he was hurting her breasts. She did not move, feeling the hot tears of relief scald her eyes and run down her nose.

'Lindy . . . Lindy-Lou . . . darling! I'm such a brute. Forgive me, dearest. It's just that I can't bear you to be cross-questioning me . . . criticizing me. What does it matter, anyhow? It's all over and done with long ago. I've no interest in her so why should you have any? I'd have expected you to be jealous . . . but to take her side and not mine . . . well, can you wonder I went off the handle?'

Of course, he's right . . . quite right, Lynn thought, allowing herself to be convinced because she wanted so much to forget this

44

nightmare of an evening. After all, even if there had been something to be said for Janet's side of the situation, there was never a broken marriage where one was all right, the other all wrong. Naturally Jerry spoke harshly of her. She'd made life pretty difficult for him and he'd been hurt. He'd probably exaggerated the bad points just as she had done to her friends. And Jerry wasn't perfect . . . no one was perfect.

'Lindy . . . Lindy . . . you do love me?'

She felt his lips against her hair, her cheek, her mouth . . . felt the ever-ready surge of her love for him, her need of him, rise to meet his insistent demands. There was no real armour against Jerry. In the end he could always weaken her every resistance by the touch of his hands; by the sweet exciting miracle of his love-making.

Why do I worry so much about him? The thought went through her head as her eyes closed and her arms went round his neck. 'Darling, darling Jerry . . . Oh, darling, I do love you so much and you know it . . . you know me so well!'

Then thought ceased and the world outside their love ceased to exist as it became no more than the core of their union.

'I love you, Lynn. I need you so much!'

'I love you, Jerry, love you . . . love you . . .'

'She really loved her first husband in spite of all he did to her.'

No, no, no?! I won't think of it. I'll never think of it again.

'Jerry, hold me tighter . . .'

Lynn's closed eyes could not shut out her fear.

* * *

'Mummy, there's someone at the front door. Can I go and see?'

She nodded her head and Sue scampered off to the front door. A moment later she was back, shyly holding Philip Castle's hand.

Lynn felt a deep blush suffuse her cheeks. This was the last man in the world she had wanted to see! She had come near to hating him last night for being the inadvertent reason for spoiling her evening. Now everything was back on a happy footing again. Jerry had left her even more affectionately than usual when he went off to the office, and she did not want to be reminded of anything to do with the past.

'I hope I've not called at an inconvenient moment?'

He looked so embarrassed standing there awkwardly, holding Sue's hand and holding his brown trilby, that her own self-consciousness departed and she tried to put him at ease.

'No . . . I mean, it's just that this is Wednesday and I'm leaving in a moment or two to fetch David . . . my son . . . from school. Wednesday's a half holiday.'

46

'What's your name?' Sue asked with a four-year-old's bluntness.

'Darling, this is Uncle Jack's brother, Uncle Philip. He's come all the way from Singapore.'

'Where's that? Did you come in a boat or in a aeroplane? David's got a aeroplane that really flies. I'll show you if you like.'

'Not now, Sue. I expect Uncle Philip would like some coffee . . . there's just time and the kettle's on. I'll tell Mary.'

'No, really, I won't stay if you're busy. I'd just thought that if you hadn't been doing anything, we might have gone out somewhere . . . I mean, I thought we might have taken Sue to the Zoo.'

Her eyes met his and they were friends again, smiling at the stupid little rhyme.

'Take Sue to the Zoo, Sue to the Zoo, Zoo to the Sue!' shouted the little girl, forgetting her shyness and dissolving into fits of laughter.

'She's very pretty!' Philip said under cover of the child's laughter. 'But not awfully like you!'

'She's like Jerry!' There was a moment's awkward silence and then he said quickly:

'Well, I'll be pushing off. Please forgive me for barging in. Nothing else to do and I thought . . .'

He was so shy, so ill-at-ease, that Lynn's heart softened. No doubt he was feeling pretty lonely, and it had been nice of him to think of taking Sue out.

47

'Look, we could come with you, to the Zoo, I mean. David would love it. He's been once, of course, but Sue's never been. That is, if you really want to be bothered with the whole family.'

His face creased into a delighted smile.

'I'd love it!' he said. 'As a matter of fact, I haven't been to the Zoo since I was a kid. I always promised myself that it would be one of the things I'd do when I got home . . . that, and Kew Gardens. I suppose one gets sentimental living abroad for a long time. One starts thinking about England in April and that kind of thing. I imagine most Brits get homesick and build up the memories, especially childhood ones.'

'I hope you won't feel let down by the factual!' Lynn said, laughing.

'I'm sure I shan't. And it's so much more fun when you have children to enjoy things with you. I mean, you get fun just out of watching them, don't you?'

He is nice, Lynn thought as she excused herself and took Sue upstairs to get her ready. I'm glad I said we'd go. It would have been silly to lose such a nice friend for no fault of his.

'Mummy, will we go in a bus? Has Uncle Philip got a car? Won't David be incited!'

They don't have very many treats, Lynn thought, combing Sue's dark hair and trying to calm the child a little. At week-ends when

48

Jerry was home he usually liked to potter round the garden, or if the weather was wet, watch the television. If they did go out, it was just the two of them.

'You need a change from the kids ... having them on your hands all week,' he always said. 'Get your gladrags on, Sweetie, and we'll go somewhere amusing!'

In a way it was nice to leave domestic life behind for a little while and just enjoy being alone with Jerry. On the other hand, weekends and their annual holiday were the only occasions Jerry saw anything much of the children and they did so adore his company. Jerry was rather losing touch with the children now. Once he used to be able to understand all their funny little self-coined words . . . their jokes . . . knew exactly how they spent their brief day and could meet them on equal footing. Now he didn't always know what they were talking about and occasionally was irritated because they, Lynn included, suddenly laughed at a joke he knew nothing of. Yet it was really his fault. He *could* give them more time. She'd talk to him about the children one evening . . .

'Mummy, will we see a really and truly elephant? Will we ride on it? Can I see the fishes in the water? David says . . .'

'Sue, we won't go at all if you don't hurry up. Let me tie those laces, now, quickly!'

She paid little attention to her own clothes,

49

leaving on her coat and skirt and just running a comb through her hair. It never occurred to her to smarten up for Philip and yet the moment she rejoined him he said observantly:

'I like the way you do your hair. It doesn't suit every woman scraped back off the face but you have such good features.'

She felt suddenly shy beneath his scrutiny and more than a little puzzled by the paradox of his character. Sometimes he could be so personal (as she had discovered already last night) and yet he was fundamentally very shy.

'I like your fringe, too, young lady!' he said, realizing that Sue was glowering at him. Her face brightened instantly and Lynn had to laugh.

'Oh, the vanity of small girls. You know, even at four Sue is very much a woman. You can turn her head any time with a nice compliment.'

'I shall marry you!' Sue announced, slipping her hand into Philip's and smiling up at him coquettishly. 'If I don't marry Tom, I mean.'

'The milkman's eleven-year-old son who helps on Saturdays!' Lynn explained. 'You're in favour, Philip. Tom is hero number one. Now I think we ought to go or David will be wondering what's happened to us.'

David was a little more reserved with his affections now at six than was Sue at four. But during the afternoon he found time to clutch Lynn's hand and say:

50

'This is great, Mummy. I do *like* Uncle Philip, don't you?'

Privately, Lynn agreed with him. Philip was quite charming. One forgot how ungainly and, well, almost ugly, he was and found oneself liking the shagginess and oddness about him. Once he forgot to be shy, he had depths in his conversation that surprised and interested Lynn. When not rioting round like a schoolboy with the children, he walked or stood beside her; answering her questions. He told her a little about himself . . . his childhood in a rambling old country house in Kent where he and four brothers had run wild until suddenly their father had collected his thoughts and packed them off for the first time to prep school. With the aid of a cane, the masters had eventually succeeded in taming them sufficiently to get them into public school, where the older boys took over with far swifter and greater effect. His four brothers had joined the R.A.F. and he himself had had to make do with the Army as his sight wasn't good enough for flying. Two of his brothers were killed in action and one in a motor cycle accident—a series of shocks which had eventually killed his mother and forced his father into retirement as soon as Philip came out of the army and was able to take his place in the family business.

'I was quite glad to get out of England,' he told her, biting the stem of his pipe. 'Somehow

51

the old house seemed terribly big and empty without Derek and Jim and Martin. Jack married Marion, as of course you know, so he'd left home, too. Father thought it would be good for me to handle things out in Singapore. I agreed . . . partly for my own feelings but also because, strangely, he seemed to miss the other boys less when none of us were there. I suppose he could make believe we were all away at school or something when the house was quite empty. With me there, he would say such things as: 'Pip, tell Derek and Martin and Jim dinner's on the table. I will not permit you boys to be late for meals . . .' Then he'd remember and he seemed to collapse for a few days. After a while he'd speak of them again, as if they were alive.'

'That's terribly sad!' Lynn said, much moved. 'What is he doing now, Philip?'

'He died at the beginning of the year. I'd heard he was seriously ill and was ready to fly home when Jack's telegram arrived saying he was dead. So I stayed on to clear things up for my successor.'

'How sad,' Lynn whispered, 'that you should not have been there with your father at the end.'

'Jack said he thought we were all there. It was the first time he'd ever spoken of us during our adult years . . . it was usually as boys he remembered us. But before he died, he spoke of Martin, Jim and Derek and of

52

me, too . . . saying how proud he was of us all. Then he told Jack he was just leaving to collect the boys from school . . . and he died.'

'Marion never told me.'

'Maybe Jack didn't tell her. We're all rather reticent about the family . . . perhaps because we were once such a perfectly happy and united household. My mother and father adored each other and us. I think the only tragedy was that they never had a girl; but in the end they said they were glad as she'd have been so spoilt by five brothers. When the first gap came in our ranks, we all tried to behave as if it hadn't happened. Mother dying finally finished things; the family could never be the same after that. I never told anyone before.'

'Thank you for telling me,' Lynn said quietly. 'Is your old home sold now?'

Philip re-lit his pipe.

'No. Maybe I'm being stupidly sentimental but when Jack and I cleared things up as executors for Father's will, we discussed putting it on the market but we couldn't do it, somehow. It was agreed that we'd keep it in the family and maybe eventually fill the house with kids again. But as you know, Jack and Marion haven't so far been too lucky about that side of their marriage. And I'm not married, so the house is eating up the interest on our capital on upkeep, repairs, taxes and so on, and remains empty. Crazy, I suppose, but I can't let it go.'

'I don't think it's crazy. Maybe one day you will live there, Philip, with an enormous family. It's possible, isn't it?'

He gave her a long, steady look which for a brief instant confused and puzzled her.

'No, I don't think it is possible now. I don't think I shall ever get married. By the way, surely it must be time for tea!'

She realized the subject was closed and they collected the children from the monkeyhouse, 'where they really belonged', Lynn said, laughing, and made for the tearooms.

Later, when she told Jerry about the afternoon and he asked her, 'What in the world did you find to talk about?' she evaded a direct reply. Somehow Philip's story of his childhood had moved her to sympathetic understanding and she knew that he would not wish her to discuss it with anyone else. Besides, she rather doubted that Jerry would, in turn, be moved.

'Anyone would think he was the only one to have deaths in the family!' She could almost imagine the tone of his voice. But it was different for Jerry . . . he'd been an only child and later, when he was grown up, his father and mother had divorced and each married again.

'Jolly good thing they did,' had been Jerry's comment. 'They never got on. It suited me down to the ground as I had two homes and both households used to kill the fatted calf when it was their turn to have me. In fact, they were constantly rivalling each other for my company!'

It hadn't been bravado, but the truth. Lynn had met Jerry's parents at their wedding and Jerry, perfectly at ease with both step-parents, had slightly shocked Lynn by saying:

'When Father heard Mother was giving us a cheque for three thousand, he doubled it. So we've quite a nice nest-egg, my sweet!'

The only child of parents she had adored and who'd longed but been unable to have a large family, Lynn knew her sympathies to be with Philip. She'd lost both parents when she was in her teens and her small world had come tumbling down about her head. She'd lived with her aunt until she was old enough to share a flat with friends, but the shock of losing her parents in adolescence had left her with a permanent feeling of insecurity.

Perhaps that is why I'm so dependent on Jerry's love, she thought as she sat watching him from her armchair where he was engrossed in the evening paper. Dear Jerry! How unfairly handsome he was with those dark eyes . . . that crop of boyish hair and that soft mouth which brought such a strange maternal feeling to her heart.

'Huh! Fool deserves to be hanged just for being so stupid!' he commented on the latest murder trial. He looked up, caught her eye and grinned, tossing her the paper.

'Read all about it. Quite entertaining. You're looking very attractive tonight.'

'I don't feel it. I feel tired,' she smiled back at him.

'We'll just sleep tonight!' Jerry grinned again. 'Nothing else but sleep!'

I love being married! Lynn thought. I love the quiet friendly intimacy of moments like these. I love you, Jerry.

She felt softened, contented, placid, not knowing yet that in her womb the fruit of last night's love-making already stirred.

CHAPTER FOUR

The children were playing happily on the floor with the box of toys Marion kept specially for them. Quite often Lynn would come here to tea after she had collected David from school and spend an hour or two in pleasant companionship with Marion before it was time to go home to put them to bed and tidy herself a little before Jerry's return.

'Cigarette?' Marion asked as they settled down more comfortably in armchairs on either side of the blazing fire. It was only October and yet already the frost was touching the evening air and the darknesss was coming more speedily to the late afternoon.

Lynn shook her head, a smile playing about

the corners of her mouth.

'I've given it up,' she announced. 'Marion, one of the things I wanted to tell you about this afternoon . . . no one else knows yet but I'm just about certain I'm having another baby!'

She waited for her friend's happy congratulations, for Marion, being childless, had always shown a deep interest in David and Sue. Lynn had taken it for granted that she would applaud this news. But even while Marion's lips said:

'Oh, darling, how wonderful for you!' there was a strange expression in her eyes. Was it concern? Lynn wondered, amazed. Surely Marion didn't think she would be unable to cope with a third child?

'I haven't told a soul yet . . . not even Jerry!' she added quickly. 'You see, I've only been more or less certain today . . . felt dreadfully sick after breakfast!'

'You . . . you and Jerry . . . planned a third . . . now?' Lynn smiled.

'Well, to be truthful . . . no! Though I shall let Aunt Meg think it was planned. She feels two is quite enough for me to look after. I wish Aunt Meg was slightly more modern in her outlook. Because she always had ample means . . . dozens of servants and Nannies and all the rest, she thinks I'm living a life of complete drudgery, but Jerry earns a good enough salary for someone of his age. He's doing well, too. As a matter of fact, Marion, he's been expecting promotion for a while now. Henderson pretty well promised him way back on David's birthday that he was going to push him up a rung. Jerry can't understand why it hasn't come through. But I know Jerry will go far; he's enormously ambitious, Marion, and clever. And Heaven knows he works hard enough. It's becoming a rarity for him to be home early these days and he's often having to stay in town the odd night, which he never did in the old days. But then they are giving him more and more responsibility and he's having to do quite a bit of entertaining.'

'Lynn, don't you think it might be better for you both if you moved to London? I mean, you're all but a grass widow these days. You must feel pretty lonely with Jerry away so much?'

Lynn sighed. It was true that the time was hanging heavy on her hands at night. The evenings dragged out interminably and she didn't care for going to the cinema on her own. At first she had rather welcomed the occasional night in which to get all her odd jobs done . . . wash her hair, perhaps, or sort out her clothes or even spend a leisurely hour in the bath after a snack supper and go to bed with a book. But now she scarcely saw Jerry except at week-ends and had begun to dread the long dark evenings alone with only the telly for company.

'I suppose it might be a good thing in some ways, but there is so much against living in London,' she answered Marion's question thoughtfully. 'Jerry and I did discuss it only the other night. But he's dead against the idea . . . says it isn't good for the children, and I do agree with him. Also it would be much more expensive; and I couldn't just turn them loose in the garden in town, could I? And then there's Jerry himself to be considered. He says it means so much to be able to get right away from his work and relax or take some exercise in some really fresh air at the week-ends.'

'I suppose you're right. Still, I can't help feeling it isn't a good thing, Lynn . . . for your marriage, I mean . . . for *you*.'

Lynn gave a puzzled frown.

'But I'm perfectly all right, Marion. I have Sue all day for company and David part of the day, too. And now there'll be a new baby to keep me busy. It's only . . .'

'That you feel you'd like more of Jerry in your life,' Marion stated as a matter of fact.

'Well, yes,' Lynn admitted. 'Much as I adore the children, I'm still just as much in love with Jerry as ever and naturally I want to be with him as long and as often as possible. But I can't very well complain. He's doing all this overtime for David and Sue and me . . . and I'm not the nagging kind of wife to stand in the way of his career. It'll be better when he gets up a bit higher. I've just got to be patient.

59

That's one of the reasons I'm so happy about this baby. It's come at the right time although neither of us actually thought about a third. It'll be good for Sue not to be the baby any longer and David will be delighted.'

'Well, I'm glad you're so pleased, darling,' Marion said truthfully. 'All the same, Lynn, I'm worried about you . . . and Jerry.'

Lynn gave a laugh of sheer amazement.

'But Marion, what on earth makes you say such a thing? We're ideally happy. Jerry is more than wonderful to me these days. What is there to worry about?'

Marion shifted uncomfortably in her chair. She was torn between her desire to protect Lynn and yet wasn't certain that evading the truth was the right way.

'Jack wormed it out of Philip that you . . . you had a bit of a tiff . . . at our party a couple of months back,' she hedged.

Lynn laughed.

'Well, that's true but that was ten weeks ago. As a matter of fact I think it was the night of your party that was responsible for this addition to the Birch family. You knew of course that Jerry's first wife was here?'

'Yes, Philip told me. I'd have warned you before you came if I'd known. Philip was dreadfully cut up about it because he felt he was responsible for spoiling your evening.'

Lynn could look back on that unfortunate affair with all but perfect equanimity. She

60

had thought the whole thing over the day after the party and realized that she had been quite stupid to make such a scene about Jane Hedges. Naturally her friends would condemn Jerry, just as his friends would have sided with him. She, Lynn, was Jerry's wife now and he loved her and she should trust him. He had never given her any cause to doubt his love and even on those occasions when he had let her down, or, as she chose to think of it, let their marriage down he had never stopped loving her. She knew she must learn sooner or later to accept the weakness in Jerry's nature just as he had to accept hers. The marriage vow itself stated 'for better or for worse' and looking at the whole affair in that way, she knew she had no real cause to worry about anything . . . so long as Jerry continued loving her.

'Philip came round next day to apologize! But I expect he told you,' Lynn said. 'It wasn't his fault and anyway, I dare say I'd have been bound to run into her sooner or later. I was silly to get so het up over the whole thing. Plenty of second wives are quite friendly with the exes. As a matter of fact I rather liked her . . . in spite of everything. But Jerry feels pretty badly about the way she treated him and for his sake I wouldn't follow up the acquaintance.'

'I . . . I liked her, too,' Marion announced . . . her voice still oddly hesitant and without her usual undertone of humour and candour. Lynn seemed unaware of it. 'I . . . that is, Jack and I . . . met her again. She and her husband and Philip . . . we all dined together last week.'

Lynn felt herself slowly tensing and wondered at the little shiver of apprehension that stole over her.

'Oh? Tell me about her, Marion.'

'There's nothing much to tell,' Marion said untruthfully. 'We never got talking intimately. She knew, of course, that I was a friend of yours so that fact alone prevented any confidences. Her husband was quite charming.'

Marion could not after all say what had lain on her mind like a burning coal ever since that evening. She could not bring herself to be the one to wipe that happy trusting smile from Lynn's unsuspecting face.

'Tell her if you want to!' Jack had advised. 'After all, forewarned is forearmed, or whatever the saying is.'

It had taken Marion a week of sleepless nights and continual thought on the subject to pluck up courage to ask Lynn round . . . for the purpose of telling her. But at the last moment she was again beaten by the thought of the effect it might have on Lynn.

'You're a friend of Mrs. Birch's, aren't you?'

Jane Hedges' soft voice had sounded oddly arresting as she and Marion sat side by side, powdering their noses in the ladies' room near the end of the evening.

'Yes, I am her closest friend. I've known her since she was at school with me.'

'I met her for a brief while at your party,' the voice continued and Marion turned at last to meet the girl's luminous dark eyes. 'I rather liked her although I had expected to find her very different and to dislike her on sight. It's . . . it's because I liked her that I made up my mind to tell you something tonight. Will you forgive me if it's rather personal?'

Before Marion could form a reply, the girl continued:

'Tell her from me not to trust him . . . Jerry, I mean. He'll lie and lie and go on lying. It's not just that he lied to me . . . but to everyone. She mustn't trust him . . . ever! I wouldn't want her to be hurt . . . the way I was hurt. Please warn her. She looked so . . . so vulnerable . . . just as I was. Will you tell her?'

Marion had been so thunderstruck that she had been speechless.

'Jack and I have known Jerry for years!' she said at last. 'We've never had cause to doubt his word. It wouldn't be fair to him to condemn him to his . . . his wife against our own judgement. We like him!'

'Yes, he's charming,' Jane Hedges agreed calmly. 'And I suppose you're right about it not being fair. But I felt I must speak . . . warn *her*. He won't be faithful and she'll be so hurt.'

Marion found that in spite of every instinct to the contrary, she could not make herself resent this unwarranted interference into her friends' personal lives. Perhaps it was because the girl spoke with such sincerity. The thought did sweep across her mind that Jerry's first wife might be activated by jealousy; but she rejected it almost instantly. There was no doubt that she was deeply attached to her second husband; her eyes followed him constantly with a warm, loving regard. And somehow Marion *knew* that she was activated by sincere motives . . . a wish to warn and protect Lynn.

'Don't you think that . . . that Jerry may have changed since you knew him?' she asked at last. 'I mean, I'm not doubting your word that he was unfaithful to you, but he could have settled down. He has settled down with Lynn. He has a happy home . . . children . . .'

'Yes . . . yes, I know. But Jerry cannot change. He has to have other women. He needs the excitement of chase and conquest and adoration to bolster him up. Underneath he's afraid . . . of his own weakness. I know him so well. He gets his self-confidence from knowing he's irresistible to other women. It's not enough to know that his wife loves him. If there isn't a physical antidote to his fears, then he falls back on drink. He's a hopeless coward. He's weak and he won't face up to his weaknesses. He'll never change.'

'I'm quite sure he isn't like that now . . . since he married Lynn,' Marion said; too

64

deeply absorbed by her own thoughts to be aware of the possible hurt she might be inflicting on the other woman.

But later, remembering, thinking, she had realized with a shock that she herself knew of three lapses in Jerry's life already. How many more might there not be that she did not know of? That even Lynn might be unaware of? She was profoundly disturbed and longed to discuss the matter with Lynn.

Instead, she could not bring herself to say anything at all.

These thoughts had rocketed swiftly through her mind in a matter of seconds. Lynn, unaware of the abyss so near her feet, said suddenly:

'I do like Jack's brother. He's a poppet. We had such a wonderful afternoon at the Zoo!'

'Oh, Pip's sweet!' agreed Marion instantly. 'As you know, he's got a flat in town now so we've only seen him once or twice. I think he's just a little bit in love with you, Lynn. You made a big hit, you know!'

Lynn laughed at the absurdity of such a remark . . . or so it seemed to her.

'Why, I haven't heard a word from him since that afternoon. I don't even know where he's living!' she said.

'No! But Jack and I think he's avoiding you on purpose. When we spoke of you, he shut up like a clam. It's my theory that he fell for you hook, line and sinker and he's doing the decent thing. Dear old Pip, he would of course!'

'Marion, you idiot! I'm sure you're quite wrong. We were good friends for a very short time and that, I dare say, was quite long enough for him. All the same, I'm sorry he has gone back to London. The children adored him and it was nice to be escorted to the Zoo! I found him such a considerate host.'

'His manners are impeccable!' Marion agreed, smiling. 'There's something a little old-fashioned and rather attractive about Pip's old-world courtesy to females. I don't know about you, but he makes me feel as if I ought to be wearing long, rustling skirts and a wide-brimmed, flower-decorated hat and carrying a parasol!'

'And take size two in shoes and have an eighteen-inch waist!' agreed Lynn, laughing. 'No, it's not fair to laugh at him, Marion. He's too nice to be joked about. I mean, I like those good manners . . . the feeling I'm being taken care of . . . that I'm breakable and must be handled with care!'

'Jack's a little the same . . . only not so much so,' said Marion. 'I dare say it's because Pip was out East so long that he didn't get blunted, or should I say toughened, by the constant example of the modern male in England today.'

Lynn remembered suddenly what Pip had told her of his home life; of the mother he had so adored. Perhaps it was this adoration for his

66

mother and his lack of sisters that had given him such a regard for the opposite sex.

'It is a shame he isn't married!' she said thoughtfully. 'He was really wonderful with David and Sue and I think he's a homey type. He'd make such a good, steady, reliable husband!'

'Perhaps that's what scares off the girls!' Marion said wisely. 'Most of us prefer a little excitement and not so much steadiness when we're "dating". Besides, poor old Pip isn't exactly an oil panting.'

'He's not unattractive!' Lynn said, laughing again. 'In an odd kind of way, he's nice . . . in the shaggy, tweedy, bearish kind of way, I mean!'

'I can quite see why he fell for you!' Marion stated. 'With that golden hair of yours and those Mona Lisa eyes you look the epitome of beautiful English womanhood at its best! One can imagine you in your garden with a basket of flowers on your arm and your pretty children draped around your skirts, looking cool and mysterious and feminine. Now one would scarcely imagine me that way . . . more like a plump washerwoman with untidy hair straggling round my hot cheeks and an enormous mountain of washing clasped to my ample bosom . . . or perhaps with a rolling-pin covered in flour.'

'Oh, nonsense, Marion!' Lynn laughed until the tears came to her eyes, and the children

67

left their toys and watched her, grinning shyly.

'What's funny, what's funny, what's funny?' Sue began to cry, dancing up and down from one foot to the other.

'It's only Aunty Marion . . .' Lynn began, when fresh laughter overwhelmed her.

'Aunt Marion's funny!' shouted the little girl. 'Look, David, Aunty Marion's funny!'

Both children were laughing now . . . David more soberly for he was by nature much more reserved and less prone to bursts of emotion than his sister.

When they had calmed down a little, Marion's maid brought in tea and later they played paper games to amuse the children. When they had gone, Marion tidied up the toys and the room seemed strangely quiet and subdued, the laughter having gone out of it and out of her mood, too. She remembered again that she had not, after all, passed on Jane Hedges' strange warning and was relieved that she had not done so. Several days had passed since she had seen her and now, without that quiet insistent voice in her ears, she could begin to doubt the truth in what was said. She wanted for Lynn's sake to disbelieve it. It was so much easier to make herself think that Jane Hedges spoke as she did because she hated Jerry and was jealous of Lynn. Far, far easier than telling Lynn what she had said.

And back home once more, Lynn was bathing the children and hurrying them a little to their beds because she wanted time to change into a pretty dress. She had planned a special dinner for Jerry tonight . . . his favourite dishes . . . and had stretched the housekeeping to a bottle of claret she knew he loved.

Tonight was to be especially wonderful. For one thing it would be their first long evening together for three days. For another, she was going to tell him later on about the new baby.

She was filled with happy, expectant exhilaration and she sang as she worked, her eyes bright and her cheeks flushed. It was wonderful to be still so much in love!

CHAPTER FIVE

At six-thirty the telephone rang. So often recently at precisely this hour Jerry had telephoned saying he would be late, that for a moment Lynn felt too sick with disappointment to bring herself to lift the receiver. This evening was to have been such a special occasion . . . the dinner . . . her news . . .

'Mummy, that's the telephone. Shall I answer it?'

David stood at the top of the stairs looking pink and scrubbed, his eyes bluer than ever as they reflected the shade of his dressing-gown.

'All right, darling!'

She stood in the kitchen where she had been heating some milk for Sue, listening to David's precise little voice giving their number and asking in his most grown-up manner who was speaking please. She waited for the inevitable 'Oh, hullo, Daddy, it's me, David!' But instead, she heard:

'Oh, hullo, Uncle Philip! . . . Yes, it's David. Did you get our letter?' (This was a combined 'thank you' from himself and Sue laboriously written and posted the day after the trip to the Zoo!) . . . 'Oh, yes, please, we'd love to. Yes, she's in the kitchen . . . I'll call her.'

A moment later he came in, his face shining with excitement.

'Uncle Philip says he'll take Sue and me down the Thames on a river boat next fine Wednesday afternoon. Isn't it smashing? We can go, can't we?'

His face fell for a moment.

'I don't *think* he said you, too, Mummy. Would you mind awfully being left behind?'

She gave him an impulsive hug, her heart singing with joy . . . partly because it was not Jerry, partly because she so loved this little son of hers who never failed to think of her pleasure, her comfort. He was more sensitive to her feelings even than Jerry.

'How nice to hear from you, Philip. Oddly enough I was at Marion's today and was saying we had not heard from you for several weeks.'

'Well, I've been fairly busy moving into my

70

new bachelor establishment and finding my way around town. I've settled in now and I thought I'd give you a ring to suggest . . . well, maybe it would be possible to see you one day soon? Are you ever in London? Maybe we could lunch together?'

How easy it was to imagine that shy smile accompanying his hesitant voice. It would be great to see him again. Once the first few moments of shyness had passed, he was such a pleasant conversationalist and it was really ages since she had been taken out to lunch.

'I'd love it, Philip. I can always get up provided I have a little notice . . . except Wednesdays of course when I like to be home with David.'

'Well, in that case, would the . . . the day after tomorrow do? At the Berkeley, one o'clock?'

'That sounds rather smart for this particular housewife!' Lynn said, smiling. 'Honestly, Philip, I'm not all that enthusiastic about these fashionable places unless you really want to go there.'

She heard his slight laugh, then his voice saying:

'To be truthful I don't. I'd rather take you to a little restaurant I know of old . . . in Soho. The food is really good and it's quiet and unpretentious. I only thought you might prefer the Berkeley.'

'You should know me better than that,

Philip!' Lynn laughed easily. 'Did I strike you as the smart young matron-about-town?'

'No . . . at least not really . . . but somehow I must have had the feeling at the back of my mind that you would look just right in one of these smart places where all the fashionable young women go!'

'I shall take that as a compliment,' Lynn stated. 'You're a tonic, Philip. I'd begun to feel rather dowdy and domesticated.'

'Domesticated, yes . . . dowdy never!'

How nice it was to be having such a silly, flirtatious conversation on the telephone! And how silly of Marion to have imagined Philip felt anything more than friendship for her! He had few if any women friends and it was quite natural that he should invite her to lunch.

'Incidentally, David told me about the river suggestion. It's very kind of you, Philip; I know they'd love it.'

'And you, too?'

'Why, yes, I would!' Lynn agreed. 'Especially if the weather is nice!'

'We can always do Madame Tussaud's as an alternative. I haven't been there since I was twelve!'

'And I've never been!' Lynn commented. 'Oh, Philip, Sue's shouting for her supper so I'd better go. Tell me where to meet you on Thursday.'

How nice! How satisfying to have 'a date' to look forward to, Lynn thought as she hurried to catch up on the last ten minutes. Jerry will tease me about my new admirer! It's a good thing he isn't the jealous type. But no one could object to Philip. He's the least dangerous man I know! Even Jerry can't have failed to notice how little of that fatal attraction there is about Philip. Compared with Jerry, no woman would consider him in a romantic light, nice as he is!

Lynn was in her bath, the children reading in their beds, when Jerry opened the front door. He was nearly an hour early and surprised them all. Lynn heard nothing till Sue ran shouting down the landing: 'Daddy, Daddy! Come and say good-night! David and me's in bed! Mummy's in the bath!'

She hurried quickly into a dressing-gown and into the warm pink-gold of her bedroom. Jerry came in smiling about fifteen minutes later as she was putting the finishing touches to her make-up.

'Um, you smell delicious!' he said, bending over and kissing the back of her neck.

She smiled at him in the triple mirror, her mind and body filled with mental and physical comfort.

'We're not going out, are we?'

'No, darling. But I've got something special for dinner so I thought I'd dress for the occasion!'

Jerry started to undo his tie and she left her dressing-table and went over to the bed to sit for a moment and talk to him.

'You're early, Jerry. What a nice surprise!'

He turned away from her as he pulled his shirt over his head. His voice came through muffled . . . mumbling something about not having seen much of her lately.

'Jerry! About your working late so often . . .'

'Yes?'

'Is it absolutely essential? I mean, it seems wrong somehow that you should have to do so much overtime and not get paid for it.'

He went across to the mirror and started to comb his hair. She looked at the broad, muscular shoulders with their faint covering of dark hair beneath the tanned shoulder blades and for a moment was swept by a wave of love for him . . . it was not just physical desire . . . but a sudden yearning of her whole body for this beautiful male body that was part of her life, her being. The emotion was as much aesthetic as physical. His shoulders were broad, his back long, his hips narrow. He was beautifully made.

For a moment, she thought of her own body . . . still perfect, slender and unaffected as yet by the new baby in her womb. She remembered her last two pregnancies and how she had come to view herself through Jerry's eyes . . . not as a woman fulfilling her natural function and therefore still beautiful; but as a cumbersome, unwieldy body, alien to him; undesirable to him! After her children's

74

births, she had done every exercise she knew, worn every support, and in a short while her figure had returned almost to normal. She had been fuller in the breasts after David, but it had suited her, Jerry said. And since she had not fed Sue herself, her measurements had remained unchanged.

For the first time, she began to wonder if Jerry would be as pleased as herself with her news. He looked upon six of those nine months as six months of her beauty denied him . . . a price he was forced to pay for the pleasure of having a son and a daughter! His tone of voice had been light enough but with an odd note of petulance about it when he had made that remark.

'Oh, let him be pleased, let him want it too!' she thought in sudden anxiety.

'. . . pay dividends in the end,' she heard him answering her last remark and realized she had missed part of his reply. 'It just has to be faced, darling, though I'll try my best to get out of it when I can. There isn't really anything I can do about it.'

'Jerry . . . suppose we lived in town? I mean you could do some entertaining at home then, couldn't you?'

He put down the comb and turned to look at her, his expression unreadable.

'Lynn, you know you don't really want to live in London. Nor do I. Nor would the kids. So let's not argue that out again.'

She sighed and stood up. Jerry was right . . . none of them really did want to live in London so it was silly to talk about it. And nothing . . . no argument . . . must spoil this evening.

'I'll go and tuck the children up and check on the dinner,' she told him, lifting her face for his kiss.

'If it tastes as good as you look I'll over-eat!' he said, touching her cheek with his lips and grinning into her eyes. 'I'll be down in a tick to mix a drink worthy of the occasion.'

The drink, the meal and their individual moods had all been perfect, Lynn reflected as later, she sat on the stool at Jerry's feet, coffee cup in hand, staring dreamily and contentedly into the fire. Jerry's fingers played idly with a curl at the nape of her neck and at last she reached over her shoulder and his hand touched and held hers.

'Perfect!' he said. 'You know, darling, we ought to have more evenings like this. I keep feeling we're celebrating something! It isn't our anniversary, is it? I can't have forgotten!'

'No, dearest! That's December!'

The half-smile left her face as she realized that this was the right moment to tell him. Strange how reluctant she was to break the enchantment of this moment.

'Jerry?'

'Uh-huh?'

'In a way it is a kind of celebration. I've some news for you. Can you take a surprise?'

'Nice one?'

'I think so! I hope you'll think so, too.'

'Well, then, fire away. I'm all attention. You know, from all this build-up you've been handing me, I'd guess from my knowledge of the feminine sex that you were about to announce the coming of the stork!'

He laughed at his joke and a moment later said:

'Sorry, sweet, if I've spoiled the moment. I just couldn't help a laugh at the thought. I mean, suppose it did happen! It could, you know. God, I'd be wild. We really ought to take more care, darling, oughtn't we? Another pair of little pattering feet would be just about the last straw.'

He seemed to have forgotten Lynn as he elaborated unknowingly on his little theme. He seemed unaware that Lynn had withdrawn her hand from his grasp; nor could he see from behind the tense expression on her face, the bitter hurt in her eyes.

'With David off to prep school in a couple of months we'll have to draw in the reins a bit,' he continued. 'And I suppose Sue will be starting kindergarten soon, too. God, how expensive everything is these days! If only income tax were down, we might keep our heads above water. As for my little bit of capital, even that's not worth its salt with the interest on it taxed, too. I say, Lynn, I'm sorry, sweet, going off at a tangent. I interrupted you.

Now tell me what we're celebrating. Six years ago to the day we were honeymooning. No, we weren't, so it isn't that! I know, six years ago today we met!'

'Jerry!' Lynn's hands clenched in her lap, but her voice was controlled. 'About what you were saying just now, Jerry, would it really be so distasteful to you to have another baby? I mean, leaving the financial side out of it for the moment, wouldn't you want a third child? I thought you were so proud . . . so pleased about David and Sue.'

'Well, I was . . . I am!' Jerry replied. 'All the same, two's enough. We've got a boy and a girl and I don't see the point of having any more mouths to feed. Good God, when I think of what we both had to go through to acquire the two we have, I shudder at the thought of a third! No, sweet, we'll just have to be a little more careful, methinks. Now, do concentrate, Lynn, and tell me if I'm right . . . did we first meet in October?'

If I speak, my voice will tremble, Lynn thought desperately as she strove to control the panic of disappointment that was now a cold hard lump where her heart should be. Yet she must tell him now before he could say worse. She should have told him right away before he could think up any reasons against a third child. At least then she might not have known that he did not want it. Yet would that make it any better? Did ignorance ever make

78

things better?

'Jerry . . . don't go on! Don't say anything for a moment or two. What I had to tell you . . . oh, darling, we *are* having another. I'm all but completely certain!'

She could not bring herself to look at his face but abruptly he swung her round so that he could look into her eyes.

'You're joking!' he said accusingly. But even as he said it, he knew it wasn't so. 'No, I refuse to believe it! When? How? It just can't be true!'

She bit her lip, trying to remain calm in the face of his questions, fired at her as if they were accusations.

'Jerry, the night of Marion's party . . . I think it must have been then. We didn't . . . oh, darling, don't look so horrified, please. If I don't mind, why should you? We'll manage somehow. After all, the promotion Henderson promised you is bound to come through soon. And . . .'

She broke off as he all but pushed her aside and stood up, his face coldly furious, and paced in front of the fire in a way that might have been comically melodramatic if the occasion hadn't been so deadly important.

'Not now . . . now of all times! God, what a fool I've been! Now . . . of all times!'

He stopped, putting his hands to his face and for a moment covering it completely.

She stood up quickly and put her arms on

his.

'Jerry, I never for a moment believed you'd take it like this. Why not now? I mean, what is particularly awful about now? We'll manage somehow, darling. Please don't be so upset about it. After all, it will help to keep me busy while you're away so much.'

He put down his hands and for a brief moment stared into her eyes. Trying to fathom his expression, Lynn could only see fear. Yet why should he be afraid?

'Jerry, if we love one another, nothing can hurt us . . . touch us. You'll see, darling, this third baby will probably be the dearest of all. Darling, try and be pleased . . . for my sake.'

She had comforted him first and now she appealed to him. Did he not see how desperately his attitude hurt her? They weren't really so hard up; by a lot of people's standards they were very well off, and Jerry's job was absolutely secure. If he got his rise, they'd be no worse off than they were now.

Oh, Jerry, darling, be pleased . . . a little bit pleased.

He turned away from her and went across to the cupboard, pulling out a bottle and pouring himself a double whisky. She sat down heavily in an armchair, watching him, overcome now with a hopeless, unaccountable fatigue. She waited for him to speak.

'Lynn!' His voice startled her, it was so harsh. His eyes stared into the half empty glass and he went again to the bottle and topped it up. 'Lynn, what you said just now . . . about really loving each other then nothing else mattered. Did you mean it?'

She was sufficiently surprised to be momentarily speechless. Then she said:

'Of course I did, darling. You know nothing else in the world matters to me but you and the children.'

'Yes! But how long will it continue to be like that? You . . . you haven't always felt that way.'

'But I have, I have!' Lynn cried amazed. 'I've never stopped loving you, Jerry, you know that.'

'Not even when . . . when you found out about my being unfaithful?'

'No!' Lynn said, her voice a whisper but the word itself hard and true. 'Not even then, Jerry. I was hurt . . . bitterly hurt, but I never stopped loving you. I don't think I could.'

Quite suddenly he was on his knees beside her, his head in her lap, his voice muffled as over and over again he called her name.

Aghast, Lynn stroked his head as she might have tried to comfort David or Sue.

'Darling, don't, please, please don't!' she whispered. 'Whatever it is, Jerry, it can't be this bad. I do love you, darling . . . with all my heart. I'm yours for as long as you need me. You know that.'

'Lynn! Something ghastly has happened. I wanted to keep it from you, but now I have got to tell you. But I'm afraid . . . afraid of losing you.'

Something touched and then slowly squeezed her heart so that her whole body became a quick, aching pain. Her face was chalk white, her lower lip scarlet where she had bitten into it with her teeth.

'Jerry . . . don't tell me if you'd rather not. You don't have to tell me anything!'

No, that was silly. Ignorance never helped anything. It was better to know.

'That's why I'm torturing myself, Lynn. I don't have to tell you but you may find out. Either way, I might lose you.'

'I won't leave you, Jerry! Not if you really want me . . . love me.'

The words were drawn from her almost involuntarily. This was the first occasion in their marriage when she had ever felt the stronger of the two. Up to now, she had always felt that Jerry was the dominant partner; the more knowledgeable, the more determined. Now she saw a new helpless side to him and it touched all that was so fundamentally maternal in her.

'Please tell me, Jerry . . . everything!'

He stood up, wiping his face with the back of his hand, and lit a cigarette. Then he walked across the room and stood by the window, looking at the back of her head. She realized that he didn't want her to see his face.

'Lynn, I'm trusting you not to go back on

what you just said . . . about leaving me, I mean. I will tell you. I must tell someone. I've been nearly crazy with anxiety. How shall I begin? It's all such a ghastly muddle. We've been so wretchedly unlucky . . .'

'You and I, Jerry, or you and someone else?'

'All of us! You see, there is someone else involved. It really began that day of Marion's party . . .' He gave a short, bitter laugh. 'A lot seems to have begun that day, doesn't it? Well, it started before that, I suppose. You remember my telling you about Henderson asking me to lunch, and his . . . niece being there, too?'

'Yes!' (So it was another woman! He had betrayed her again!)

'Well, I had met her before. You see, I realized she might be useful to me, Lynn, help me up the ladder a bit, Henderson being her uncle. So I took her out once or twice and, well . . . well, she began to fall in love with me. I realized it of course but thought I'd play around a bit and avoid getting seriously involved. It was just a flirtation, Lynn, no more than that, I swear it. Then one evening she told me she'd arranged this lunch and naturally I was grateful; so when she asked me back to her flat, I went . . . just to please her. I mean, I was grateful and I didn't want to seem boorish. Anyway, we had a few drinks and men . . . then it happened. Lynn, I swear it only happened

83

once. I never meant it to happen at all. You must see that; believe me. She was really to blame . . . started telling me how much she loved me and that . . . that kind of thing. Next thing I knew she was half undressed and well, I lost my head. You see how it all happened? You do understand, Lynn?'

'I understand what you are saying, Jerry, and why you were afraid to tell me about it.'

(How strange her voice sounded.)

'Yes, naturally, I was. But Lynn, what really made me afraid was that something happened that night. I mean . . . well, she's going to have a baby. If Henderson ever found out, I'd be sacked on the spot. She won't tell, of course. She's promised me not to. But you can't trust anyone. And she's pretty scared. That's why I've been so late home so often lately. I haven't been working. I've been with her trying to work things out. I thought I'd got everything fixed, then . . . then you tell me about this baby you're having.'

'So what have you arranged?'

Lynn could hardly believe that her voice sounded so normal. They could have been discussing an everyday event. She was unaware of the rigid tenseness of her body.

'Well, I was paying for her to go abroad once the . . . the baby starts to show. That's why any other expense at this time is so much a disaster. Then later, after it's born she's going to get it adopted.'

'You mean, she isn't going to look after it herself?'

In spite of everything, Lynn found herself thinking: I could never give a child of mine away!

'What else can she do? I can't marry her; she knows that. She knew from the beginning . . . well, almost the beginning . . . that I was married. And Henderson's her only relative. He'd cut off her allowance like that'—he snapped his fingers—'if he ever learned the truth. He's terribly old-fashioned. He was even tricky about my divorce, as I told you.'

'But Jerry, it's your child, too!'

It hurt desperately to say it.

'Don't for Heaven's sake keep harping on it. I know it's mine. Do you think I'm proud of the fact?'

'No . . . no, I suppose not!' Funny, how detached she seemed to be . . . as if they were discussing other people, not themselves. Was it because she herself was carrying a new life within her that all she could really feel to be important now was this other life?

'It wouldn't be easy starting again if Henderson does get hold of the truth. I'll be out on my ear. We'd be in a nice enough fix, Lynn, without still another mouth to feed.'

Strange how his confidence seemed to be returning. The note of pleading had temporarily vanished. Was it because she had not so far offered any condemnation?

'Lynn! I know this must be a ghastly shock to you!' He was beside her now, reaching for her hand. But she drew it away as if his touch burned her. His mouth tightened and he turned back and poured himself another drink.

Whisky won't help you Jerry, she thought: Will I? What can I do? Do I still love him after all? Can I love a man who will do this to me? To his children? Jerry . . . oh, Jerry!

'Henderson had better not find out if only for David's and Sue's sake . . . and the new baby's. For their sakes, I'll help you, Jerry, if I can.'

'But there's nothing you can do, Lynn. Nothing anyone can do. Marcia refuses utterly to try to get rid of the baby.'

I'm glad, I'm glad! thought Lynn. I've never, ever believed that abortion was right, and it's Jerry's child, related through him to David, and to Sue.

'Maybe I can do something. If Henderson began to get at all suspicious, we could have him to dinner; let him see we're . . . united; that nothing is wrong.'

A look of triumph came into his eyes which she did not see.

'Lynn, can you ever forgive me? I don't deserve anyone like you. I never wanted it to happen . . . you do understand, don't you? I've never loved anyone else in the world but you!'

'Not even Jane? Janet?'

He was momentarily taken aback.

'Well, that was different. I mean, I was married to her so I suppose I must have loved her once. But you're the only one who really matters; you and the children.'

She stood up, her face white, her hands trembling.

'Don't talk of them. Don't ever include them in this, Jerry!'

He could involve her but not the children. She would not have them associated even indirectly with this . . . this degradation.

'I'm sorry, Lynn . . . desperately sorry. I can only hope now that we get away with it. Marcia is as anxious as I am to keep it hushed up.'

'Is this why you told me, Jerry? Were you afraid I might somehow learn the truth and divorce you? Then Henderson, too, would know the truth. But you bound me first before you told me . . . bound me with a promise not to leave you. I'm glad you haven't asked me if I still love you. I couldn't answer that question now. I think at this moment I hate you, Jerry. They say that hate is akin to love but it doesn't feel like it. I'm going to bed now. We'll talk more about it in the morning. No, tomorrow evening. Perhaps by then I'll have it all straight in my mind. Good night!'

'Lynn, don't go; don't leave me!'

She pretended not to hear him, and evading his outstretched hand, walked past him out of the room.

Jerry turned slowly and poured himself

another drink.

CHAPTER SIX

Lynn went about her usual morning activities in a daze. Even Sue noticed how absent-minded she was and remarked:

'Are you asleep with your eyes open, Mummy?'

With an effort, she forced herself to concentrate on her shopping list and later preparing lunch before she collected David from school. She felt desperately in need of a few hours' complete solitude in order to straighten things in her mind. Last night she had lain awake, turning things over with all the hopeless indetermination and confusion of utter tiredness. She had fallen asleep in the end by telling herself that a new day would bring a clearer view of events. It was unfortunate that today should be David's half-holiday.

The rather dull, cloudy weather had cleared a little by the time David came home and when he suggested an afternoon in the gardens, a combination of playground and park, Lynn eagerly agreed.

She sat alone on a bench in the half-hearted sunlight, her eyes following the children's movements but not really seeing them. She could only see the devastation of her life . . . and theirs.

If I hadn't promised, I would divorce him, she told herself for the hundredth time since last night. But deep in her heart, she knew that it wasn't just that one rash promise which held her. So much more counted when a woman was making up her mind whether to leave her husband.

First and foremost, she would be denying the children a father and plunging them in the thoroughly unpleasant position of divided loyalties. It must be best for them to have a proper home life and two parents. She would get custody, of course, but that would not prevent Jerry having access.

Lynn felt her hands tremble and clenched them tighter in her lap. That it should have come to the point where she could really look upon her own marriage in the terms of divorce laws . . . court proceedings was all but unbearable. Was this the sole result of six years of loving Jerry?

She bit her lip, trying to remain calm within herself. She did not want to remember at this moment Jerry's pleading voice when he had come to bed; nor her own disgust that he'd reached the 'maudlin' stage of drunkenness brought on by too many whiskies. She had felt for the second time in her life revolted by the man she loved; no, the third time. Drunkenness was quite abhorrent to her and she felt the same reaction as when she had heard of Jerry's previous act of unfaithfulness to her . . . that she could not bear him to touch her.

She had feigned sleep, knowing that he knew she was awake. He tried once to touch her, but she steeled her nerves so that she did not recoil and presently, the deep, drugged sleep, the effect of too much alcohol, claimed him abruptly, leaving her alone with her thoughts.

Barely a word had passed between them during breakfast. It had always been tacitly understood that they should never 'have words' in front of the children. As he rose to leave for work she made some excuse and went upstairs to avoid his good-bye kiss.

By the time he returned this evening . . . and surely he could not under any circumstances be 'working late' tonight! . . . she must have her mind made up as to her own feelings. This tension between them could not go on as it was, with its strain on her nerves. Either she must tell him she was leaving, or that she was willing to make a fresh start.

Was it really better for the children to have a father like Jerry than no father at all? Was he not a terribly bad example to David? The boy might be young now but he was growing up, and sooner or later he would see the weakness in Jerry's character. Would he be affected? At least it was some comfort to her that she did not set any great store by heredity. She had always believed that moral weakness, moral strength, was something a child acquired during the process of growing up. Belief in right and wrong and the willingness to live by those beliefs were instilled into a child, so that he either maintained those standards for himself, or lost them. Such things were an attitude of mind, not physical attributes that could be passed on through the bloodstream from parent to child.

How weak was Jerry—this man she had loved so very much? Was he really so bad? Could there not be some excuse for his behaviour? Not every man was faced with the temptations Jerry had. She had told herself all this before . . . the last time. He was so attractive to women that they would always run after him. Could he be blamed so much because, just once in a while, he weakened? He had sworn that he had not been having a steady love-affair with this Henderson girl; that it had been only once, when he'd had too much to drink. At least he had been honest enough to tell her. But had he really meant to tell her? Had he wanted to 'confess' because he was so ashamed and could not bear the lie between them? Or had he been motivated by the fear that she might find out? Did he know her so well that he had weighed up the pros and cons and decided he would be more than likely to get away with it if he threw himself on

91

her mercy? Appealed to her pity?

She shuddered. However bad Jerry was he could not always be activated by baser motives. Were he really bad through and through, surely some instinct would have told her . . . prevented her marrying him . . . loving him? Could she know so little about the real Jerry after six intimate years as his wife? Maybe I'm just beginning to learn, she told herself bitterly.

I don't really want to leave him! she thought. My life would be meaningless . . . empty without him.

Yet she would have the children. Could she support three children herself? She would have to work . . . and what could she do? Her only qualifications were an ability to paint mediocre water colours and A level passes in English and history. Neither seemed likely to lead to a job which would provide for a family of four! Of course, Jerry would have to pay a third of his income; yet there might be no income if she divorced him, for then Henderson would learn the truth and sack him.

This was the right way to think . . . practically, not emotionally. Yet in the end it was only emotion which prompted her thoughts. Deep in her heart she knew she was finding excuses to stay; to forgive; to try and forget and to go on in the hope of regaining her waning respect for the man she loved.

But it wasn't easy to forgive. It wasn't easy to think of Jerry making love to another woman only a few hours before he held her, his wife, in his arms. It was hardest of all to know that while she carried Jerry's child, another woman was doing the same; that these two unborn babies were actually related and would be born within a short time of each other; both of them unintended, unwanted, the result of unguarded passion without love. Yet it wasn't true! She did want her child in spite of everything; in spite of it being Jerry's child, too. And she could not in her heart believe that Jerry had not always loved her. That other baby might have been the result of passing physical passion, but not hers. Jerry did love her . . . and only her. She was his wife, not his mistress.

For the first time, Lynn found herself thinking of that other woman, pitying her a little. Seductress she might be, yet she must be suffering for it now. And she could not be altogether bad since she had resolved to give her baby the chance of life. There could be no consolation for her; no feeling that it must come right in the end; no man's love to guide and help her. All she had to take her through the next months was Jerry's offer of money. Otherwise she would be unprotected.

There is someone worse off than I am. There is always someone worse off than oneself, Lynn thought with faint, wry comfort.

I can be sorry now for *her* . . . more sorry for her than I am for myself; and sorriest of all for that unborn baby. It will have but a few weeks in its mother's arms and then be abandoned to the care of strangers awaiting adoption.

For one wild moment, Lynn thought of Marion who had not so long ago spoken of adopting a baby. Then she threw the idea away. Marion had not really meant it; she felt she was too old now and that she and Jack were too set in their ways to begin a family.

Not even Marion must know of this last degradation. Her own, very real pride caused her to shrink from the thought of Marion's pity. There was something else, too; some primitive instinct that fought against the thought of another woman caring for Jerry's child. That was her privilege, her right, her duty . . .

'No, no, that I cannot, would not do!'

Lynn pulled herself up sharply, realizing that she had spoken aloud and another woman sitting at the opposite end of the bench had turned to look at her curiously. There was a moment of acute embarrassment while their eyes met and then suddenly, to Lynn's confusion, the woman spoke:

'Forgive my intrusion, but are you feeling all right?'

It was a cultured, kind voice. The woman looked to be in her forties. She had an indeterminate kind of face, neither pretty nor ugly, young nor old. She was a typical middle-class woman enjoying the last of the autumn sunshine.

'Yes, thank you. I'm afraid I was thinking aloud! I . . . I sometimes do!'

The woman smiled.

'Then that's all right. You'll forgive me, I hope, but you looked so pale and tired, I thought perhaps . . .'

'No, I'm not ill,' Lynn said quickly. And on impulse, she added: 'I'm having another baby and I expect that's why I look so pale. I always feel rather sick at first.'

'Then this isn't the first time!'

'Oh, no! Those are my two children . . . over there by the swings.'

'I see them! I was watching them earlier. They're very pretty children but not a bit alike, are they?'

'No, they aren't very alike. Sue, my little girl, is like my husband!'

'My little boy was dark, rather like your little girl, he was. I . . . I lost him from leukemia when he was five years old.'

'I'm so sorry!' (Here was someone worse off even than herself or that other woman.) They were such inadequate, futile words yet she spoke them again: 'I'm so sorry!'

'My husband died a year later so I lost them both. Your little girl reminded me of Noel.'

So she was quite alone. Fate had robbed her of husband and child, too.

'Life can be very cruel!' Lynn said gently.

'You're very fortunate. It seems strange that you should be looking so sad when you have so much. Have you been bereaved lately?'

Lynn was shaken by the question as much as by the observation that had preceded it. The woman must have misjudged her surprise for she added quickly:

'Please forgive me. I'm being personal again. You see, not having anyone of my own to worry about, I find myself nosing my way into other people's lives. It's a bad habit I try hard to control. I must be the worrying kind, I think. Please forgive me!'

Lynn acted on impulse and put out her hand and touched the gloved one of this strange acquaintance.

'There's nothing to forgive. I don't think it's such a bad habit. I think you are just very maternal and can't help 'mothering' people. It's really a comfort to think that a complete stranger can worry about you. I've never really had anyone to worry about me. It's funny but that thought never occurred to me before. You see, I lost my parents when I was a girl. I lived with an aunt but somehow we never really became very close. I expect it was my fault. I probably resented her as a substitute for my own mother and after a little while she must have given up trying to win my affection. She was always kind to me. But I never told her my troubles.'

'Then your life hasn't been all happy?' Suddenly the woman smiled, her eyes lighting her face so that for a moment she did look pretty. 'There I go again. I think I'm incurable!'

Lynn smiled, too. Then the smile faded as she said:

'Not, not all happy. As a matter of fact, I'm going through rather a difficult time at the moment!' The impulse to confide was becoming increasingly difficult to control. Common sense and a natural reticence forbade discussing the most private and personal of all details of her life to anyone else, let alone a stranger. Yet that same impersonal unreal isolation of someone unknown . . . unnamed, that had caused this stranger to confide in her, was perhaps responsible also for her wish to unburden her mind.

'I expect it will all come right, my dear! I'm sure you will do the right thing. You have such a very beautiful face I don't think you could be capable of doing wrong, whatever the reasons.'

'I'm not like that. I know I have my faults. It's just that I don't know at this moment what is the right thing to do!' The soft grey eyes regarded her with sympathy.

'My dear, I think we always know somewhere deep in our hearts what is right and what is wrong. It's just that we don't always want to listen to what our hearts tell us. You know, I was faced with perhaps the most difficult of all decisions when I lost my husband and child. I wanted so much to die, too. I meant to do it. It's right that I should go, too, I told myself. No one would blame me. No one is left to care if I die or not. I wouldn't be harming anyone. There's nothing in the world to prevent me joining my loved ones. Yet all the time I knew it was wrong. Deep down inside me I knew it was wrong. Maybe it was some religious teaching which was fighting inside me for recognition. My vicar told me afterwards that he believed God Himself had stayed my hand. I don't know if he was right. I have never regained my faith. I think I 'stayed' my own hand. At the last moment, I knew it was wrong; that I must live out my allotted years; that there might be some other purpose that would make the continuance of my life worth while. I am convinced, you see, that we all have a purpose here on earth, even if at times we cannot recognise it. Our feelings can so easily blind us to our true convictions.'

'Then you believe that if one could only be guided by convictions, free of any emotions or desires, one must inevitably make the right decision?'

'Yes, I do believe that. It's a matter of being true to yourself, isn't it—*"To thine own self be true then cans't thou be not false to any man"*'

Lynn nodded. 'I think my trouble is that I don't know any more what are my convictions.

I thought I knew, but I've just learned that they were mostly quite unfounded.'

'Perhaps they weren't. Perhaps you only think so. But it is very easy to confuse instinct with conviction. Instinct . . . particularly a woman's instinct . . . can often be wrong if it is influenced by emotion. A conviction is a belief that nothing can destroy, nothing and nobody.'

'You mean, something elemental such as one's belief that it is wrong to ill-treat a child?'

'Exactly! You take my point. Nothing and nobody could make you lift your hand and brutally strike a child.'

'Yes, yes, I see. But that is a negative conviction. One can nearly always enumerate the things one must *not* do. But what about the things one ought to do? It's not so easy.'

'But surely there are only two alternatives to everything in life? If you know something is wrong, then the opposite must be right. If it is wrong to lie, it is right to tell the truth; and so on. You need only be sure of one alternative to be certain of the other.'

'But life isn't always a case of black and white. There is so often grey, too.'

'Ah, yes, indeed. Then it is not so easy. But there is another cliché I can give you that helps with the "grey" . . . that nothing stands still. It gets better or it gets worse just as it gets lighter and darker, earlier and later. Sooner or later the grey will veer towards black or white. Then you can again be sure.'

Lynn was absorbed in this conversation so completely that her companion had to draw her attention to the fact that David and Sue were standing but a few yards away watching them.

'Oh, darlings!' she said, gathering her thoughts with an effort from the abstract to the present. 'I expect you're hungry.'

'It's four o'clock, Mummy!' David said seriously. 'I heard the clock strike. And Sue and me have finished playing.'

'We'll go home to tea right away!' Lynn said. She turned back to her companion and held out her hand.

'You've been very kind and I've so much enjoyed your conversation. Do you think we might meet again sometime? Perhaps you would come to tea with us?'

'I would like that very much. I, too, have enjoyed our discussion. Good-bye for now, my dear. Good-bye, children. Enjoy your tea!'

She waved to them as they walked off. It wasn't until David said:

'Who was that, Mummy?' that Lynn realized she had not asked her companion's name nor yet her address. Unless they met again here, she might not see her again to follow up her invitation.

'Run back quickly, darling, and ask that lady to write her name and address down for me.'

She waited with Sue in the gathering twilight, drawing the little girl's coat round

100

her against the chill wind that seemed to have replaced the warmth of the afternoon air. David came back breathlessly in a moment or two.

'She'd gone, Mummy. I looked everywhere, but I couldn't see her. I 'spect she went out by the other gate and got a bus or something.'

Lynn looked back for a brief second and then turned again with a sigh.

'Oh, we'll probably run into her again here,' she said. 'It doesn't really matter.'

All the same, she could not help the feeling that she had lost something important. And at the same time, she felt faintly relieved.

Her daily help had tea waiting for them by the cheerful blaze of the sitting-room fire. As Lynn poured out the tea, she realized that she had still no idea as to how she would greet Jerry when he came home in an hour or two. Panic gripped her at her own hopeless indecision. She was only certain of one thing . . . she could not face an evening alone with Jerry, the future still unresolved and that appealing, helpless look in Jerry's eyes every time she moved away from his touch.

She jumped up and hurried out to the kitchen.

'Mary, dear, would it be possible for you to stay on for a little time this evening? I have to go out rather urgently.'

'Why, of course, Mrs. Birch. Shall I see to Mr. Birch's supper? I could put the children to bed if you want to go now!'

Dear Mary! How obliging she was . . . what a treasure!

'No, I'll pack them off early myself, thank you, Mary. It's very kind of you and I do appreciate it.'

The children were in bed by six-thirty. Suddenly panicky in case Jerry should take an early train home, Lynn hurried into a warm coat and with a last request to Mary to read to the children and have their lights out by seven if Jerry wasn't home, she slammed the front door behind her. Her feet directed her to the bus stop; although she was still uncertain where she would go, she would get on a bus as far as the station and take a train to London. She could go to her aunt's club where she would get a quiet meal by herself without fear of interruption, then think things out at her leisure, or at least until the last train home.

She regretted now that she had not left a note for Jerry just in case he should ring up Marion or her other friends to try and locate her. But there would be time when she got to London to telephone home and speak to Jerry.

It was cold and cheerless in the train. British Rail did not seem to think it necessary as yet to start the heating. In spite of the weather, they must wait until the specified date, however cold their passengers might be! It was almost too cold to think and Lynn began to doubt the wisdom of this odd impulse. She would have been far warmer, far more sensible, to stay at home; except that Jerry would have been there, she reminded herself. She could not think clearly with Jerry there.

It did not seem long before she was in town. She hurried out of the train into a telephone booth and rang her home number. Mary answered.

'Yes, Mr. Birch is home. He's saying good-night to the children. Hold on, please.'

While she waited for Jerry to come, Lynn idly leafed through the London telephone directory. What millions upon millions of names there were in these massive volumes . . . A, B, C, D . . . I wonder if the Donaldsons are still living in that studio . . . E, F, G, H, Harris, Hemlock, Henderson, Henry . . .

She nearly dropped the receiver as she tried to stop the page slipping past her finger. The book slammed shut and fell to the floor, and a second later she heard Jerry's voice:

'Lynn? What on earth's happened? I've been worried to death . . .'

'Nothing's the matter, Jerry!' she cut him short. His concern for her seemed not to touch her at all. It was as if she were, momentarily at least, numb to any feeling but the desire to retrieve that book. 'I just thought I'd like an evening by myself. I'm going to my aunt's club . . . you know the one. I'll be home on the last train.'

'But, Lynn, you can't . . .'

'I'll see you later, Jerry!' she said, and biting her lip, she put down the receiver. She had never cut him off in her life before.

A moment later she picked up the book and, with flushed cheeks and trembling hands, leafed quickly through the pages. Ah, there it was. H . . . Ha, He, Hed . . . Hen . . . Henderson. She ran her finger carefully down the initials and found what she was looking for . . . *Henderson, Marcia Miss; 8, Drayten Mews, S.W.3. Ken. 33894.*

I needn't give my name . . . just see if she's there. She's probably out anyway, then I can't see her. I'll leave it to Fate.

She dialled the number, her heart beating double pace, as the ringing tone throbbed in her ear.

She's out after all . . . Lynn thought.

'Hullo! Kensington 33894.'

'Oh, yes, is Miss Henderson in?'

I'll ring off while they are finding her. I can't do this . . . 'Miss Henderson speaking. Is that you, June?'

A cultured, soft voice, with a clear note of surprise. I can say it's a wrong number. No, I asked for her by name . . .

'No . . . I mean, my name is Mrs. Birch, Lynn Birch!' She couldn't go on. For a few moments, the line hummed. Then the girl at the other end said faintly:

'Oh!'

She was committed now . . . she must go

104

through with it, thought Lynn.

'I . . . I rather wanted to see you; that is, if you're alone.'

'Yes, I am, but excuse me, did you say Mrs. Birch?'

'I'm Jerry's wife. He isn't with me. It doesn't matter if it isn't convenient. I'm sorry I troubled you.'

'No . . . no, don't go. As a matter of fact, I am alone. It's okay by me if you want to come round. I suppose you know my address. Will you come right away?'

'I'll take a taxi now!' Lynn said, and before she lost her nerve completely, she rang off.

She'll be far more nervous than I am! she told herself as she sat in the taxi that took her nearer and nearer to the woman she had never met but who had assumed such a vital importance in her life. But what shall I say to her? Why do I want to see her? It won't do either of us any good for me to lose my temper and tell her what I think of her. Yet that is not what I want. I've no wish to abuse her; just to talk to her; see her; see if I can understand Jerry . . . make sense out of chaos.

Marcia Henderson lived in a tiny mews flat, converted as so many of them were from what were once stables. Lynn stood in front of the yellow-painted door and with a mental effort pressed her finger on the bell.

She was totally unprepared for the girl who opened it. Somewhere in the back of her mind, in her inner consciousness, she had expected Marcia Henderson to be dark . . . as Jane Hedges was dark, tiny, glowing; as was that other woman with whom Jerry had betrayed her; she too had been dark-eyed, dark-haired.

But not Marcia Henderson. This girl was tall, slender, golden-haired, blue-eyed; and, yes, she could see it, bore the most striking resemblance to herself.

CHAPTER SEVEN

'Will you come up, please?'

Lynn followed her up the narrow stairway into the tiny hall. She noticed vaguely that the flat looked very warm and inviting; was nicely furnished. Was it here that Jerry had . . . but no! She wouldn't think of that part of it now.

The two women sat down opposite one another in comfortable armchairs. Lynn declined a drink and drew a deep breath.

'Jerry told me about you. That's why I'm here!'

Her words tumbled out spontaneously. Marcia Henderson twisted her hands in her lap nervously.

'I see!' was all she said.

'I wanted to see you. He doesn't know I have come, of course.'

There was a moment's silence, then Marcia

106

said slowly: 'How . . . much . . . did . . . he tell you?'

'Everything, I suppose!' Lynn answered frankly. 'I knew that you fell in love with him; that one evening he . . . you . . . that now you're going to have a baby!' (How strange that she could work up no feeling of dislike for the woman who had harmed her so deeply. She could only feel pity for the white, stricken face that watched her own.)

'I see!' said Marcia again. 'I . . . I suppose you hate me. Are you . . . are you going to divorce your husband?'

'No!' (Until this moment, she had not known the answer to that question.) 'No, I'm not going to take any kind of action against Jerry. You see, I have two children to consider, and I, too, am going to have a baby.'

Marcia gave a little cry of surprise mingled with distress.

'Oh, no! Jerry never told me.'

'He didn't know himself until last night. That was when he told me . . . about you.'

The girl suddenly put her hands over her face and a moment later she was sobbing quietly, hopelessly. Lynn's instinct was to go to her but she could not bear the thought of any physical contact between them.

'Please don't cry. It won't make matters any better and you'll make yourself ill.'

'I'm so ashamed . . . so dreadfully ashamed. You must believe me, Mrs. Birch. When I first met Jerry, I never knew he was married. I didn't know until later . . . until it was too late. I'd always thought . . . hoped he might fall in love with me . . . marry me. I suppose I talked myself into thinking he . . . he did care. Otherwise I would never, never have . . . oh, I'm so utterly ashamed of myself!'

'You mustn't take all the blame! This isn't the first time, you know.' (She had never believed herself capable of offering her past shame as comfort to the girl who had shamed her this time.)

The tear-filled blue eyes looked up into hers, unbelievingly.

'Then . . . then you don't think that I . . . I ever intended to try to take your husband from you? I would never have tried to come between any man and his wife. I didn't know I was harming anyone else.'

'You thought like Jerry that I would not know about it and what I didn't know wouldn't hurt me?' Lynn's voice was harsh now and filled with bitterness.

'But that's not true! I didn't know . . .' She broke off suddenly, her eyes dropping to her hands that now twisted her handkerchief meaninglessly. So Jerry had let his wife think that all the time she, Marcia, had known of his wife. He hadn't confessed that it wasn't until long after he had become her lover that he had told her he was married.

'It needn't make any difference, Marcia, dear.
108

Lynn never asks questions. And I don't suppose she would care very much if she did know. She's very modern in her outlook.'

He had painted the picture of a hard, modern, sophisticated woman who led her own life and was quite willing to let Jerry lead his; who didn't really love him, but who wouldn't of course, set him free to marry anyone else because she was mildly fond of him. Marcia was no fool, and after the first few moments of conversation with Lynn she had realized that Jerry had lied. He had lied in letting Lynn imagine that Marcia had always known he was married; had lied in letting her, Marcia, believe that his wife wouldn't care.

'It needn't make any difference,' he had said to her. Had he not known how deeply, desperately, hopelessly she was in love with him by then? Had he not seen for himself in her eyes, her behaviour, that she longed every time he spoke to her for him to say he wanted to marry *her*! It had been a tremble shock to learn he was already married; even more of a shock to realize what kind of man he really was; that in spite of his marriage he was still anxious to go on coming to see her whenever the opportunity occurred; that he could never, never have loved her. That was the greatest lie of all . . . letting her think he had cared.

But what good would it serve to tell all this to his wife? She had said she did not intend to divorce him. She must love him to be able to forgive him, or at least care so much for the unity of her family that she was willing to forgive and make a fresh start. It would not do her, Marcia, much good; maybe vindicate her in Lynn's eyes, but at the cost of her own last chance of happiness. She had harmed this woman unknowingly and she would not do so again deliberately. She could keep the whole truth from her and protect her . . . make some reparation.

These thoughts flashed through her mind in a matter of seconds. Aware now that Lynn was waiting for her to explain her last remark, she said quickly:

'It wasn't like that. I . . . I didn't think of you. I suppose that sounds horribly selfish but . . . I loved him. I just couldn't help myself. I know you must hate me dreadfully, and believe me, I hate myself. If it's any comfort to you, I'm paying the price now.'

'You mean the baby?' Lynn misinterpreted Marcia's words. 'Yes, I suppose that is price. But it isn't exactly a comfort to me. It may sound strange but the thought of your baby has hurt me far more than the knowledge of Jerry's unfaithfulness. What will happen? That is what I have kept asking myself. What will happen to you? To the baby? To all of us, and most of all to my children, if the truth ever comes out?'

'Nobody will know!' Marcia said swiftly. 'I give you my most solemn promise that I

110

will never tell a soul. I'll swear that it is some other man's child. I won't let your husband's name be mentioned if ever anyone, my uncle, learned what was happening to me. I shall go away. Jerry . . . your husband . . . is helping me financially to go abroad. I'll stay away until after the baby is born.'

'Won't your uncle wonder where you have found the money to take such a prolonged holiday?'

Marcia bit her lip.

'I had thought of that. He may ask questions. I'll tell him I'm getting a job there.'

'So one lie leads to another . . . and another! So much deception!' Lynn spoke her thoughts aloud.

Marcia suddenly leant forward and touched Lynn's knee.

'Believe me, Mrs. Birch, if there was any way at all that you'd prefer, I'll fall in with your wishes. I only want now to try to make amends. Please believe that. If . . . if *you* ask me to, I'll have an abortion . . .'

'No!' Lynn cried sharply. 'I would never want that. It's wrong. It's against nature and it can be dangerous. I . . . I'm glad you haven't allowed Jerry to persuade you to such measures.'

Marcia's hands went again to her face but this time she was not weeping. Her voice was tired . . . and so low that Lynn had to strain to catch the words.

'I've been so desperate lately that once or twice I've wondered if, after all, that wasn't best.'

'No!' Lynn said again sharply. 'It isn't for Jerry to decide what is right for you or your child. If there were no other alternative, then believe me, I'd rather divorce him.'

'I wouldn't marry him . . . not even if he were free!' Marcia cried vehemently. 'Not even for the child's sake . . . *not now*. I want only to be able to start again; to try to forget all this.'

'You mean, to have the baby adopted?'

'Yes, I couldn't keep it the way I'd want. I couldn't earn enough. And of course, my uncle would find out. That would be dangerous for you and your husband. I don't want a baby and an unwanted child with no father can never have a happy home life. Its best chance of happiness is adoption.'

'It's . . . Jerry's child!' Lynn again spoke her thoughts aloud. She had never for a moment doubted this fact and now she had met Marcia she would never doubt it. This girl was fundamentally decent. She had been weak because she had fallen in love. Women in love are always weak. She, Lynn, knew only too well how fatally attractive Jerry could be. No, Marcia did not in any way strike her as being promiscuous and she believed what she had heard from her lips.

'Jerry doesn't want to be involved in any way.'

112

'Yes, he told me. You must be feeling very lonely right now. I don't hate you, Marcia. I just feel sorry for you. How old are you?'

'Twenty-five! I am old enough to know better than to land myself in this mess!'

'Is any age a weapon against love? I don't think so myself . . . not for a woman, anyway. But at least you are young enough to begin again when this is all over. You can look forward to a better future. Have you money of your own?'

'I get a small allowance from my uncle, and . . .' she broke off, biting her lip.

'Jerry has promised financial assistance?' Lynn helped her out.

The girl nodded her head, the fair hair falling across her face with the movement. She added quickly:

'But I can't take it now . . . not now.'

'That would be silly! Refusing Jerry's help won't make things any different for me, and you are entitled to it. You'll need money; it can make things so much easier for you. You must take what he offers you, and if it is not enough, you are to let me know. If you prefer, think that I am saying this because it is for my own benefit. If you have your baby somewhere abroad, then the safety of my marriage is secure.'

'But that was not what you were thinking of when you said . . . oh, Mrs. Birch, I'd give anything to undo all this. Since I met you, I

113

have realized how greatly I've injured you. I know I have no right to ask your forgiveness but at least try not to remember me too harshly.'

'Don't say any more!' Lynn said sharply now as she stood up. 'I don't blame you any more. Jerry is a good deal older than you, and far more experienced. He should not have allowed this to happen.'

'But you will forgive him? You still love him?'

'I don't know how I feel about him. But I shall keep my marriage secure . . . if that is possible.'

'I swear on my most solemn word of honour that you will never have cause to be afraid of me. You'll never hear from me again, and no one will ever know it was Jerry's child, I promise.'

Lynn stood up, her face white and tired.

'Thank you! I'm glad now that I came. I hope things are not too difficult for you.'

Marcia jumped to her feet and for a moment clasped Lynn's cool hand in hers.

'I shall never forget you . . . never. I shall always be sorry for what I have done.'

'Don't spend your life regretting your past. You must look to the future as I am trying to do.' Lynn held out her hand and for a brief moment her eyes smiled. 'Good-bye . . . and good luck.'

What good has it done me to meet her?

she asked herself as she walked along the now frosty streets towards Kensington tube station. She intended going to the little snack bar nearby to have a meal before returning home. There was no purpose in going to Aunt Meg's Club now for it was nearly nine o'clock.

No good, perhaps, she told herself truthfully, but I'm glad I went. In many ways, she reminded me of myself when Jerry married me. Was that what attracted him? At least it would be a comfort to me if I could believe it. What makes a man unfaithful to his wife? In books, films, articles, one is always being told it is the wife's own fault. Somewhere she has failed him; she has failed to keep him attracted to her. Yet I never nag Jerry, and he has told me often that he still finds me beautiful. Nor could he simulate the physical feeling he has had for me. Why has he need of it from other women, too? I don't understand! Is it really my fault?

These thoughts and others fled through her mind as her body automatically took her to the Pelham Grill where she ordered a light meal. Was it Jerry's home life that somehow or other irked him to get away from domesticity for brief spells? Did the children tire or bore or aggravate him? Did she herself fail to give him companionship; understanding?

She could not find an answer that provided a real excuse for Jerry. He saw too little of David and Sue for them to be the cause.

And he loved them; she was certain of that. She herself listened always to his accounts of his day's work, his worries, his hopes, his ambitions, and offered advice or sympathy when either was due. She had never yet refused to accompany him to any party or outing, even if she had not really wanted to go. Mostly she loved anything that kept her in Jerry's company; and she was so often told by her friends how beautifully she dressed—how pretty she was.

In spite of the fact that they had seemed so perfectly matched in every way, he had twice been unfaithful to her. And there was Jane, his first wife; the woman who had divorced him. Did a woman ever divorce her husband without just cause? Not if she loved him, and Philip had said that Jane had once loved Jerry. What was wrong with Jerry? With herself? With their marriage?

It crossed her mind briefly that maybe Jerry was one of those people who could not say 'no'; one of those men who could not resist temptation. But she rejected the idea for Jerry had never seemed to her to be a weak character. He played the dominant part in their marriage; made the decisions, acted on them, carried out their plans; he ordered and she obeyed although not in a negative way for she had a strong will of her own. But while she loved him, his will was really always hers, too, except in very minor differences of opinion.

Nobody ever thought of talking about Lynn's husband. It was 'Jerry's wife . . . you know, the girl who's married to that charming, good-looking fellow over there!' He was immensely popular with all her friends. Yet he had never appeared conceited.

It did not occur to Lynn that his bouts of excessive drinking indicated a basic weakness in his character. She believed them to have been a childish exhibition of bad temper. On each occasion he had been in the wrong, and getting drunk, because he knew how much she hated it, was his act of self-defence; his attack back on her.

He won't be unfaithful again! she thought now. After this, he'll never dare to go to another woman. He must know that I wouldn't stand for it again. I'd leave him then divorce him and take the children. If I go home now and tell him this, quietly, as a matter of plain fact, he will know I mean it and that knowledge will help him to resist temptation next time. Maybe I was too weak, too ineffectual in dealing with the last time. He knew all along that I loved him far too much to leave him whatever he had done. Well, now it will be different . . . and he'll know it. It was really not unlike dealing over a point of discipline with David! She had learned to her cost that to let a major offence go virtually unpunished invariably brought a second occasion.

Reducing the whole affair to such trivial

similarities both helped and comforted her. She could tell herself now that in so many ways Jerry—and perhaps other men, too—were still little boys at heart. Men did not seem ever quite to grow out of their boyhood in the way that girls became women and matured in every way.

In the train going home, Lynn found herself feeling almost sorry for Jerry. Poor darling, he'll be worried to death right now. I've never walked out of the house before without telling him where I was going, what to do! And I won't tell him where I have been. I don't think Marcia Henderson will tell him either. I'll tell him the conclusions I have come to; what I think of him; and maybe in a day or two we can begin to behave normally again. I cannot bear there to be anything between us. In spite of everything, I still love him. It is the greater part of my life, my love for my husband.

She realized with a little shock of surprise that she could still love Jerry even when she had lost some of her respect for him. She did not know that her love had ceased to be part of her very being and was now only a thought firmly fixed by her will in her mind.

CHAPTER EIGHT

It was the faint aroma of liver and bacon
coming from the kitchen, where Mary was
preparing the children's lunch, that first
brought back to Lynn's disturbed mind the
fact that she had forgotten something vital. A
second later, she remembered what it was—
her lunch date with Philip.

'Oh, how frightful!' she said aloud, her hand
covering her mouth as she realized that it was
an impossibility now to arrive anywhere near
one o'clock.

Sue looked up from the floor where she was
carefully sorting her dolls' clothes and asked:

'What's the matter, Mummy?' Have you
forgotten something?'

'Yes!' Lynn gasped. 'Now be a good girl,
darling, and play by yourself for a moment or
two. I must go and telephone Aunty Marion.'

Maybe Marion would know the number of
Philip's office or his home. At worst she could
ring the Soho restaurant and leave a message
for him. What an awful thing to have done!
Yet with last night and its prior events, she had
been robbed of all thought but the mechanical
ones that prompted her daily domestic routine.
As she had made the beds, ironed, dusted, her
mind had been exclusively on Jerry; on the
eager way he had greeted her return the night

119

before. She had let him make her a cup of tea and when they were sitting quietly together by the fire he had maintained for her, she had told him that she intended to stay by him, stay with him.

How forcefully he had pleaded for her forgiveness; for the chance to prove that the future would be quite different from the past! How many times he had re-iterated that he loved her and only her; that it was all a ghastly mistake and that he knew he had behaved unforgivably. She had never doubted his sincerity for no man could have been more sincere in his regrets or in his wish to make a fresh start. He had convinced her utterly that he was bitterly ashamed for what he had done to her, and that he meant it when he said it would never, never happen again.

I must have faith in him, she had told herself as she listened to his protestations. I must not lose that or our future is a hopeless one.

So she told him that she thought it would be a good plan in a day or two to arrange an evening in town with Henderson; to let him see how 'united' they were lest any suspicion had crossed his mind that all was not well. Jerry jumped at the idea and the colour seemed to come back to his face, the assurance to his tone of voice, as she outlined her idea. If the worst came to the worst and Henderson did discover that Jerry had been having an affair with his niece, then she, Lynn, would deny it absolutely; tell Henderson that Jerry had come home every evening and that there could have been no opportunity for an affair. What Lynn did not tell Jerry was that Marcia had promised never to disclose the truth. It would not do Jerry any harm to suffer a little for the pain he had inflicted on them all. Meanwhile she had told him that she wished him to send Marcia a generous cheque to see her through the next months and at the same time write to her to say that it was her, Lynn's, wish that she should accept it. He was also to tell her in the letter that he had decided it was the fairest thing to all of them not to see her again.

'When that is done, Jerry,' she'd added, 'we'll try to make a fresh start; to forget all this. But you must give me a little time. Don't expect too much from me for a little while!'

'I know I can't expect you to love me now after this,' he had said. 'But I'll do everything in my power to win your respect again, Lynn. I couldn't bear to go on without your love. You mean far too much to me. You're my life . . . you and the children. I know it must be difficult for you to believe this after what I have done, but it is true. You believe it in your heart, don't you?'

'Yes. I think I do believe it,' she had admitted. 'You see, I could not go on with our marriage if I didn't think that was true.'

As if aware of her wishes, Jerry had not

121

tried to kiss her good-night and had gone quietly to the spare bedroom where he had slept during her last confinement, and where either of them always slept if the other were ill. She knew that he would await her indication that he could return to their own large double bedroom, and that when she did this, she would be prepared for a complete reconciliation.

Small wonder that she had forgotten Philip! Yet she knew it was unforgivable of her.

'What on earth shall I do, Marion? I don't want to hurt his feelings and yet I don't see what else I can say.'

'Why not let me telephone his office and say you're in bed with a touch of 'flu and have asked me to ring for you? You're such a hopeless liar, darling!'

'Oh, Marion, would you? It would be a white lie. I know I would hate to think that someone thought so little of an invitation of mine as to forget it completely!'

She rang off, partly relieved that Marion was providing her with an excuse but still upset at the thought that she had been not only forgetful but thoroughly bad-mannered into the bargain.

Sue was taking her afternoon nap and Lynn was in the sitting-room writing a letter to her aunt when the front door-bell rang.

A moment later Mary came in with an enormous bunch of bronze chrysanthemums and said:

'There's a gentleman wishes to see you if you're well enough, Madam. I didn't rightly understand him but he seemed to think you were in bed.'

Philip! Lynn thought as the colour left her cheeks to be replaced by a more than guilty flush. Her first inclination was to refuse to see him; to tell Mary to say she was not well enough. But her innate honesty got the better of her. She might have done it if Philip had not been Philip. But here he was, come all the way from London to see her, believing Marion's story. The least she could do would be to see him now.

'Show him in, Mary. And perhaps you'd better bring some coffee!'

She stood up as Philip came in, a look of surprise on his face.

'My dear, I'm so glad to see you up! I gathered from Marion that you were laid low with this 'flu. I know how depressing it can be so I thought I'd run down for a few minutes to cheer you up.'

'Philip, you make me feel perfectly awful!' she said as she sat down opposite him. There was nothing for it now but to confess. 'You've been so kind to come and I've behaved so badly.'

He looked at her directly, suddenly understanding. 'You mean you got Marion to cancel the luncheon? That you aren't really ill?'

There was so much distress in his voice that Lynn felt she was being justly punished for her casual behaviour. She realised now that Philip had set a good deal more store by her lunch date than their very new friendship warranted; that the thought of being with her was important to him. She was not vain enough to be pleased . . . only concerned that if Philip ever became seriously fond of her their friendship would have to come to an end.

'No, I'm not ill,' she said truthfully, looking down at her hands. 'But Philip, please don't think I didn't want to see you. I did. I was looking forward to it very much indeed. Then . . . then something happened. I had rather a nasty shock, and because of that I forgot our date. I didn't want to hurt your feelings by appearing so casual so I let Marion tell a lie for me. I realize now that I shouldn't have done that. I'm very sorry.'

'It wasn't necessary!' the man said quietly, not looking at her. 'If you'd told me the truth, I would have understood.'

'Yes, I realise that now! I'd forgotten how understanding a person you are. But you see, I couldn't tell you what had happened to make me forget. I thought . . . oh, I don't know what I thought. I just acted without thinking. Please forgive me, Philip.'

He stood up quickly.

'Of course. I'll push off now. I expect you

have a lot to do.'

She jumped up and impulsively laid a hand on his arm. She could not let him go like that . . . obviously very hurt, and even perhaps not believing that she had had good reason to forget a luncheon.

'No, don't go, Philip, please! I've nothing at all to do. I'll only sit around and brood by myself. Please stay! You see, I've only just this moment realized it but you're the one person in the world I'd really *like* to see this afternoon.'

The sincerity in her voice must have convinced him for he smiled that sudden quick smile which so transformed his rugged face, and sat down again.

'You know, you don't look well, Lynn. If you'd told me you'd just got up from your sick-bed, I'd have believed you!'

'You make me ashamed!' Lynn said truthfully. 'I expect I just look tired!'

'No, you look ill!' he persisted.

Lynn felt suddenly shy.

'Perhaps that's because I'm having another baby!'

She avoided his eyes and so did not see the look of pain in them. His voice when he spoke was a little over-emphasized.

'I'm so glad to hear your good news. You must be very pleased!'

She bit her lip. After all, was she pleased? She had been! But somehow Jerry's confession

125

had destroyed all pleasure in her baby; indeed she had scarcely thought about it again until now. Would she ever be able to dissociate her child once it was born from this crisis in her marriage? This fresh blow to her pride? She forgot suddenly that she had imagined Philip might be growing too fond of her; forgot the fact that he was virtually a stranger; forgot everything but her need to confide in someone. Until now, she had had to bottle up her emotions, suffer all the shock inside her.

The relief of telling someone would be so enormous that she felt she must now do so. There was something so warm and sympathetic about this man. One felt he might so easily be an elder brother; that he would always be calm, sensible, fair, in his attitude to life and people that any confidence would be completely safe with him. She knew this without having to ask herself why she should believe in his integrity so completely.

'Coffee, Mrs Birch!'

'Thank you, Mary! Philip, you have had some lunch?' For a moment their eyes met and they smiled. Then he said:

'Yes, I had a snack before I came here. But I'd love some coffee.'

Mary left them and with Lynn's permission, Philip lit a pipe.

'You didn't answer my question,' he said at last into the silence that had fallen. 'But perhaps it needs no answer. Of course you are

126

pleased!'

'No, not "of course". You see, until last night I wasn't sure if I wanted to . . . divorce Jerry!' She had not meant to say so much and yet now it was said, she was glad. Even as she spoke the words, she knew how untrue they were. She had had no intention of divorcing Jerry. She had never seriously contemplated a life without him. She had never really stopped loving him.

'I don't understand! I thought you were so much in love with him. The other night . . .'

'Yes! I do love my husband. But . . . well, there's another woman in the picture . . . or was! I didn't know about it till the day before yesterday. It was this this business that made me forget our lunch!'

'My dear, I'm terribly sorry. But I find it hard to believe. I just can't imagine any man with you as his wife looking at another woman!'

Lynn smiled a trifle wryly.

'Thank you for that! All the same, you aren't married, Philip. I don't suppose any one of us is perfect and I dare say Jerry's unfaithfulness is partly my fault. I've probably failed him somewhere. Otherwise he wouldn't have had to find something else in someone else, would he?'

'It depends what he wanted. I mean, why he did what he did! I cannot believe you failed him.'

127

'It's over now,' Lynn said shortly, 'but it has spoilt my pleasure in discovering I am to have another baby. I suppose it all sounds rather degrading to you!'

'My dear, nothing you did would ever sound degrading to me. And I am more surprised than anything else that this should have happened to you of all people.'

'Why not to me? It happens to thousands of women, doesn't it?'

'Yes, I suppose so. But you struck me as someone who had made marriage a kind of career; that it was your sole interest in life.'

'That makes me sound rather dull!'

'Does it? Perhaps I'm old-fashioned but that's what I first admired in you—your enthusiasm for your home and children and husband.'

'You're very comforting, Philip. But I don't think I have been very intelligent. I have given up my life to my home and family and husband because it is what I have always most wanted to do. I've tried to make a happy home but I can't have been very much good at it, in spite of what you say, since I have failed.'

He leant forward in his chair, studying her face and seeing the bitterness, the hurt in her eyes.

'I don't think *you* have failed. And I don't think you really believe that either.'

'Perhaps it is easier to believe it. Preferable at least to believing one's husband has failed.

Do you think me very disloyal talking of him like this? I know I shouldn't be doing so but . . . well, I have no one else to talk to. Marion is my only close friend and I could not have told her. I couldn't bear her to start disliking Jerry.'

'But you don't mind if I do?' He gave a wry smile. 'One could take it that because I mean nothing at all to you, what I think is of equal unimportance.'

He was only half serious and yet she felt she had to correct him.

'That wasn't the reason, Philip. Let me at least make up with some honesty now for the lie earlier! The truth is I feel you're somehow impartial. Perhaps it is because you have not been a part of my life before now and are therefore not in any way involved as Marion and Jack are, for instance.'

'An outsider?'

'Perhaps in one way. But in another way, I feel strangely that we've known each other for years and that you're the most trusted friend I have. I don't really know what makes me talk like this. I just can't help it!'

'That is good enough reason. And you *can* trust me, Lynn. I have no need to say that anything you told me will remain between ourselves. I think sometimes one has to confide in other people. One's thoughts, worries can become too much to contain in one's heart. Perhaps long ago, people could go and talk things over with their priest . . . or vicar. Nowadays one doesn't discuss one's personal life with people like that because religion and the modern way of life seem so far apart.'

'But they shouldn't be!' Lynn cried.

'No. But they are, aren't they? Once in a while one does meet the kind of clergyman one could talk to. But not often. Maybe it is because for one thing the Church doesn't recognize divorce even though English law does. It seems to put them outside our modern society. One knows that they are bound by their own teaching to advise people to stick together whatever the provocation.'

'All the same, I do in part agree with them,' Lynn said hesitantly. 'I think a lot of people don't take their marriage vows seriously enough. We say "for better or for worse" but we are not prepared to take the bad when it comes along.'

'Granted! Nevertheless, there are limits to the amount of "bad" any person can live with. I'm not for a moment suggesting yours is such a case. But there must be a certain amount of willingness on *both* sides, mustn't there? No one can go on trying to make a marriage succeed if the other partner has ceased to try or to care.'

'I think I believe that, too. So long as they both want to make a go of it, then the marriage should continue. That's why I'm not divorcing

Jerry. He's very remorseful and he's sworn it will never happen again. I don't think that I could face it again.'

He was silent for a few minutes. Then he said quietly: 'You know, don't you, that if ever that should happen I'd like you to continue to look on me as a friend.'

In spite of the seriousness of his words, she smiled.

'Oh, Philip, don't be so pessimistic. I sincerely hope it isn't going to happen again. Believe me, I don't think I've been through such a bad moment in my life before.' She remembered suddenly those three other occasions when she had had good cause to doubt Jerry . . . even to hate him, and her eyes clouded. 'I want so much to be able to live happily ever after, Philip. Don't you think that's ever possible?'

'Yes, I think it is possible. I hope and pray it will be so for you, too. Look, my dear, may I tell *you* something now? You won't be offended?'

For a brief second she hesitated, some innermost instinct warning her that she might not want to hear his confession. Then she nodded her head.

'It's just this piece of advice . . . it may be quite wrong advice at that,' he said quietly, not looking at her. 'But for all it's worth, don't let your Jerry see quite how much you love him.'

Lynn gave a start of surprise . . . and could

131

it have been disappointment, too? Had she imagined for one wild moment that he, Philip, was about to tell her he cared for her more than as a friend? But no! She would not have wanted that for it would have meant an end to their friendship, and she had only just begun to value it seriously.

'I don't know why you say that, Philip. I'm not even sure that I do still love Jerry as much as I once did.'

'But my dear, you do! In your heart you do. I could not help seeing your face that night when at last he turned up at Marion's party. It was . . . well, fulfilled! No woman looks like you did unless she cares.'

'But that was before I knew about . . .'

'Don't you know in your heart that if I told you now I had come here to announce the fact that he's left you, you'd feel your life was broken into small pieces? You couldn't forgive him so readily if you loved him less.'

Lynn bit her lip, a faint colour stealing into her cheeks.

'I suppose that is true. But I have been near to hating him, too!'

'So is love akin to hate!'

Lynn held out her hands in a strange mute appeal. The gesture touched the man who was now watching her changing expressions, and for a moment he glanced away from those uncertain, unhappy eyes.

'Philip, why must I not let him know how

deeply I do care? I'm his wife! Surely after six years of married life it shouldn't be necessary to play that game "don't be too sure of me"?'

'I think that depends on the man. Some like always to feel they are hunting a quarry, for want of a better expression. They take for granted what is given them too easily. There is no victory in accepting a never-ending, never-varying generosity of heart; of affection.'

'But I couldn't hide my feelings!' Lynn cried spontaneously. 'If you'd ever been in love, you'd know it isn't possible to conceal that fact from the other person!' She broke off suddenly, realizing what she had said. 'Philip, I'm sorry. Perhaps too much thinking has turned my brain a little. I expect you have been in love; you must have been to be so understanding.'

'Only once, but I shall love her always,' Philip said quietly.

Lynn felt a purely feminine second of jealousy. How stupid of her to imagine that he should have felt especially fond of *her*.

'Was it someone you were unable to marry?'

'Yes. She has a husband.'

Lynn longed to hear more about this woman but Philip seemed disinclined to continue the conversation. She supposed it was someone in Singapore.

'Are you saying, then, that if you had married her, you wouldn't have wanted to be too certain of her affections?'

133

'No!' There was no hesitation in his voice. 'But then, I am no doubt a very different type of character from your husband. I like to be sure of myself and others. I like security. Perhaps I'm silly but I would never put one foot in front of the other unless I was certain the ground was firm and solid in front of me! Too cautious, I expect. Or else a coward. At any rate, I should consider myself the happiest man on earth if my wife loved me as you love your husband. But I suspect it isn't the best way for him. Keep him guessing a little. Make him earn a little of that love you give him.'

Lynn smiled in spite of the seriousness of the conversation.

'Don't overrate me, Philip. I'm not always the loving, devoted wife. I'm sure Jerry wouldn't agree that I give him too much affection!'

'I don't believe you ever denied him anything he wanted!'

'Oh, Philip! What a thing to say!'

'Isn't it true?'

'I don't know. I suppose if I'm honest I'd agree that it wouldn't be easy to say no to Jerry.' Her voice became bitter for a moment as she added, 'I don't think it's very easy for any woman to say no to him.'

'All the more reason for you to be different from the rest.'

'But I'm his wife!'

'Yes, I know. I know it isn't easy; but it

can be done. Believe me, I am speaking from experience. It *is* possible to conceal the extent of one's emotions.'

As I am concealing mine from you at this moment, he thought with strange savageness. You do not know that it is you who I love. I thought this could not happen to me; that I was immune to such depths of romantic love! I thought myself beyond that helpless, hopeless, all-powerful emotion; imagined that it was not for me. Yet I didn't know you before, did I, my beautiful Lynn!

She is the only really selfless woman I know, he told himself thoughtfully, I have watched so many of them in my thirty-eight years betraying in the end their selfishness, pettiness, vanity. I suppose I've disliked most women I've known at all well. And now I love one woman who is perfect and she can never be mine! Even if she learns one day what a worthless chap she has married, she wouldn't look at me. For the first time in my life I can envy another man's looks; charm; whatever it is Birch has that appeals so much to her. For her sake I hope she never knows the truth about him; for her sake I'll try to help her keep him. But for my own I would gladly kill him!

He remembered suddenly that Lynn was at this moment carrying Birch's child and a completely new emotion assailed him, purest jealousy. He knew deep down that he would have given anything to know that it was his child she would bear; his, Philip Castle's. This was the one woman in the world whom he would wish to be the mother of his children. Instead she was the mother to two of Jerry Birch's children.

I should dislike them! he thought, yet knew this was not the case. He loved all children, and David and Sue were part of Lynn. For that he loved them especially dearly. And now there was to be another baby.

'Lynn, I have no children of my own to spoil. Would you let me be a godfather to your new baby?'

She had not expected those words after the silence that had fallen and she gave a surprised smile.

'Philip! You really are an extraordinary person. On the surface you seem so orderly, yet your remark seems to me, at any rate, to be quite inconsequential! Yes, of course you can be a godfather!'

He smiled and, as always, she could not restrain that feeling of surprise to see his face so transformed from the ugly to the attractive.

'Still waters run deep! I hope I shall remain a mystery to you, Lynn.'

'But I am not a mystery to you, Philip. You know far too much about me already!'

'It is good for friends to know each other well. We will be good friends, my dear?'

'Yes, please!' Lynn cried, childishly it seemed to her but with a warmth that caused the man's heart to beat faster.

'And it is a lovely idea your being a godfather. I'm flattered that you should suggest it.'

Philip stood up.

'On that satisfactory note, I shall depart!' he said. 'Thank you for giving me so much of your time, and don't worry, my dear.'

'You've been wonderfully kind!' Lynn said, holding out her hand. 'I didn't deserve it and I'm all the more grateful because of that. May we meet again soon? Or have I forfeited my right to suggest it?'

'You must always feel free to ask anything you want of me. I'm a very lonely, rather dull old bachelor and your company would cheer me up enormously whenever you can find a spare moment for me. And that applies to the children, too.'

'Then I'll ring you soon, Philip. And thank you again!'

I wish there were more I could do, he thought as he walked away from the house. I wish . . . but what's the use of wishing? I must be content with her friendship and at times, her company. That is something to make life worthwhile.

He wondered how it was he had never before realized that life was empty and meaningless without love. He had known only that he was lonely and blamed his broken home life for that. But he knew now that even had his mother and father been alive, and his brothers, too, none would have filled the void in his heart. Only Lynn could do that . . . Lynn, who had married a man who wasn't worth her single glance.

I'll kill him if he hurts her again! he thought, and then, smiling at his own surprising emotions, he tried to turn his mind back to his work.

CHAPTER NINE

She lay in the nursing-home bed feeling drowsy and perfectly content. At the foot of the bed in his tiny crib lay her baby son. He was twenty-four hours old and she had just fed him.

I'm so happy, she thought for the hundredth time. This is really the happiest time of my whole life.

The baby, Paul, had been born easily and without any real pain. Jerry had insisted that she come to this nursing-home although she knew it was costing him a great deal of money and she had argued with him about it for several weeks. But he had wanted her to have a real rest and she knew, too, that he wanted to spoil her.

Ever since that unhappy day when she had told him about Paul for the first time,

Jerry had done everything any man could do to make up for it. All through the long and sometimes trying months that she had carried Paul, Jerry had been a model husband . . . solicitous, adoring, patient, full of little attentions which meant such a lot. Every night he came home with some little gift . . . a bunch of violets, a box of chocolates, a jar of ginger. He remembered all her fancies from previous pregnancies, and added his own charming thoughts as well. No woman could have asked for a more perfect husband.

I'm so lucky! she thought. I have everything in the world I want. And to think that seven months ago I was wondering whether I ought to divorce Jerry!

For a brief moment her thoughts were clouded. It was not after all possible to forget *everything* that had so upset her life then. There was always in the background the nagging memory of Marcia Henderson. Had she had *her* baby? Where was she? Was she being as well looked after as herself? But no! That was not possible. She would be hard up, and probably as unhappy as any woman could be at this moment. She had neither the comfort of Jerry's love nor the comfort which his money had brought her, his wife!

If only I knew that she was all right! Lynn told herself with a sigh, I should be able to forget her. But I can't ask Jerry and he wouldn't know. There's no way of finding out now.

Her thoughts were interrupted by a knock on the door. One of the younger nurses came in.

'There's a gentleman to see you, Mrs. Birch . . . a Mr. Castle. I took these from him in case you did not feel up to seeing him just yet. Poor man; he looked so embarrassed by this armful!'

She displayed a gigantic bunch of white lilac and narcissi.

'Oh, how lovely!' Lynn said. 'I'll see him, Nurse. The baby is to be his godchild, you know. I expect it's really him he wants to see!'

A moment later, Philip came into the room looking suddenly much taller and larger and generally more cumbersome than she had remembered him from their last luncheon several weeks ago.

'Philip! Thank you for the lovely flowers. They're beautiful!'

He gave her an awkward smile, and turning away from her, he bent over the cot.

'So this is my godchild! My goodness, Lynn, he's nearly bald! I thought babies had hair when they were born!'

'Not always!' Lynn laughed. 'Isn't he beautiful?'

Philip studied the baby more closely.

'Yes, I think he is, in a way. First time I looked he seemed rather like a little monkey. Now I can see just the very faintest

140

resemblance to you.

Lynn laughed outright and after a moment of horror, when he realized how badly he had expressed himself, Philip laughed, too.

'Well, you know what I meant, Lynn. How are you? You look wonderfully well!'

'I am!' she said as he sat down beside her, a huge great bear of a man in the small room. 'And I'm so happy, Philip. Life seems wonderful to me.'

'Have the children seen the baby yet?'

'They came this morning with Jerry just for a peep! David said he looked like a monkey, too! But Sue thought he was perfect. She can't wait for me to get home and let her help me bath him. I've promised she shall put the powder on. David is looking further ahead and has promised to lend him his football boots as he's turned out to be a boy after all. I think he rather expected a girl and he's pleased it's Paul and not Pauline!'

'So am I! I always wanted . . .'

'A son?' Lynn asked gently when he broke off. 'Dear Philip, you should get married you know and have a son of your own.'

'You know that isn't possible, Lynn. In any case, I'm much too old to be a father now!'

'Rubbish!' Lynn laughed. 'You're not forty yet, are you? And older men always make the best fathers. They have more patience!'

'I'm quite happy with my new godson!' Philip said quickly. 'Now tell me, Lynn, is there anything I can get for you? Do for you?'

'I have everything . . .' Lynn began, when suddenly she had an idea. Impulsively, she said: 'Well, there is one thing, Philip. I don't know if I ought to ask you or even if I ought to . . . to do this. But it's been worrying me a little and I thought maybe you . . .

'Anything at all, Lynn. Out with it!'

He was quite unprepared for her astonishing request that he should somehow find out what had happened to Marcia Henderson and make sure she was all right.

'But my dear, is that wise? After all, she is not your responsibility.'

'But Philip, I know she was having her baby nearly the same time as I was to have Paul. I can't help thinking about her having to go through all this for the first time without anyone to help her. She couldn't tell her family because of me. They would have guessed Jerry was the father because they knew she had been seeing him. Her uncle is Jerry's boss and would have sacked him if he knew.'

'She has no money?'

Lynn bit her lip.

'Jerry sent her a cheque. It should have been enough. But I would like to be sure she is all right! And I can't ask Jerry because I made him promise never to see her or communicate with her again, so . . .'

'I'll do it if you want me to, Lynn, you know that.'

142

'Thank you, Philip. I don't know where she is now. But I can give you her last address. She may have gone abroad. She intended to have the baby adopted so I know they will both be all right once she's out of hospital. I just want to make sure, that's all!'

Philip noted the address on a slip of paper and put it in his wallet. Then as he held her hand for a brief moment before he left, she said:

'Do you think it's very silly of me, Philip?'

'Yes. But I admire you for your magnaminity, Lynn, and . . .' he could not say how much he loved her for it, too. 'Only one woman in a million would have shouldered her husband's responsibilities, or indeed felt any pity for the other woman. I'll let you know what I find out.'

After he had gone, Lynn relaxed on her pillows and felt utterly at peace. She knew she could rely on Philip. He had proved himself such a good friend. It was strange that Jerry should so dislike him but at least it was not often necessary for them to meet. Philip liked to take the children out occasionally on an afternoon jaunt . . . to the circus when Christmas had come and to the pantomime and an ice show. Occasionally she lunched with him alone. But he never came to see them during the evenings or at week-ends and she assumed this to be because he was tactful enough to realize that she treasured these hours alone with Jerry. It was easy for Philip, who was his own boss in a family firm, to take an afternoon off when he wished; but Jerry had been promoted at last and was working hard all day. He never worked late now and it was tacitly understood that this had never been so but had been an excuse to see Marcia.

When Jerry arrived to see her an hour later, Lynn could not help but ask him what was uppermost in her mind at that moment . . . why he disliked Philip.

'I don't know, sweetheart!' he said, sitting beside her bed and holding her hand as he played idly with her fingertips. 'Perhaps I'm just suspicious of his intentions. After all, it does seem a bit odd, the way he takes the kids around and brings you these . . .' He indicated Philip's flowers with a nod of his head.

Lynn smiled.

'I do believe you're jealous!' she teased him.

'Well, what if I am?'

'Nothing at all, darling!' Lynn said happily. 'It's just silly, that's all. After all, what woman would look at poor old Philip with you around? You should be sorry for him, Jerry. He's in love with some girl he can't marry and he's lonely. He'd have liked children of his own and ours are the next best thing.'

'Well, you said all that before when you persuaded me to agree to his being godfather to young Paul. Let's have a look at the little chap. Why, I do believe he's grown since last night!'

Lynn watched him with her heart so full of love that it felt to her to be aching. Tenderness for this man she loved so much brought tears to her eyes, and turning back to her, he saw them.

'Lynn, darling! What's wrong? What's the matter, my sweet?'

She clung to him weakly, half-laughing, half-crying.

'Nothing in the world. That's why I'm crying!' she whispered. 'I'm so happy, Jerry . . . so wonderfully happy; and I love you so much!'

'Silly girl!' he said, kissing the tip of her nose. 'I'll be in trouble when that nurse of yours comes in and sees you've been crying. She'll think I'm a brute!'

'So you are!' Lynn smiled through her tears. 'Oh, Jerry, I can't wait to get home again. I miss you all so much. Are the children being good with Betty?'

'Little angels. That girl seems to have a way with children.'

'I think so, too. She's really nice and they took to her right away. I thought it might not be a bad idea to see if she would be free to come on our summer holiday this year. It would leave us a bit of free time to be together, wouldn't it?'

'Splendid idea!' Jerry sounded suitably enthusiastic and Lynn felt a fresh wave of contentment. She loved being with the children at the seaside, and Jerry did, too. But it was sometimes tiresome to have to stay in night after night because they had no baby-minder, and Jerry in particular liked to be able to get away from the house for a while. If they took Betty, then they could go out as often as they wished.

After Jerry had gone, Lynn lay thinking about the young girl she had engaged to look after David and Sue while she was in the nursing-home. Jerry had at first favoured the plan of sending them both to Marion, but in the end she had persuaded him to her viewpoint. It would be so much less work for everyone if the children could remain in their home. The girl could come a week before the baby was due and stay on for a month after she, Lynn, returned from the nursing home. It would give her a chance to regain her full strength. She had been immensely lucky to find anyone so young and efficient.

Remembering the first time she had interviewed her, Lynn recalled that her immediate impression had been that the girl was too young. But after talking to her for a little while, she discovered that although she was only twenty-two, she had had a nursery nurse's training and had held two posts, as a mother's help, and had excellent references. She was a well-educated girl from a good home and Lynn felt that this was just the right person she would wish to look after the children . . . not too strict but quiet and firm and ready to play with the children on their own level.

Her mind shied now at the nasty little thought that had made her hesitate a moment longer before engaging her. Betty Smart was far from unattractive, with short curly brown hair and rather fawn-like slanting brown eyes and a pretty *retroussé* nose. Lynn had not been able to prevent that moment of doubt about Jerry . . . would he find her attractive? Possible temptation? Angrily she had rejected the thought and, hating herself for her lack of faith in Jerry, had promptly told the girl she was to come.

Jerry had proved himself in every way since that last affair. She had no doubts at all that he was more than sorry for the unhappiness he had caused and was bitterly ashamed of himself. She could at least do him the honour of having a little faith in him. After all, if Jerry ever questioned why she did not engage the girl, could he come to the conclusion that if she were going to mistrust him, he might as well be hanged for a sheep as for a lamb!

As if to back up her judgment, and her faith in Jerry, he had not shown the slightest interest in Betty during the week she, Lynn, had been with them. The girl took her evening meal with the children and so he saw little of her, but even when they did meet, Jerry was no more than polite. And when she questioned him as to what he thought of her, he merely replied that she seemed to be popular with the kids, and that was all.

'By the way, Lynn, Mary sent her "respects", and said could she come to see Baby on her half day next Wednesday,' Jerry was saying now. 'She's delighted that he's another boy and hopes you are keeping well.'

Lynn thought of her dumpy, homely daily help with affection. Dear Mary! She was so reliable and had been with them since the first year they were married. She adored the children and was a good cook when Lynn did not feel like cooking herself.

Everything in my life is perfect! she thought, smiling at herself as she reached out and touched the edge of the wooden chair beside the bed. It was always difficult to ignore superstition when anything was going well. One felt always that perfection could not last and one must take even this most stupid of precautions against taking happiness too much for granted.

'Tell me about you, Jerry!' she said, holding out her hand so that he took it automatically in his own and played with her fingertips.

'Nothing much to tell, really, Sweetheart! Working hard as usual. The boys shoved me off to the pub at lunch time and made me stand them all drinks to celebrate! Oh, yes, I saw Marion and Jack last night for a drink on the way home. Marion's coming in to see you tomorrow. Otherwise it's just work, home, eat, T.V. and bed. I miss you darling.'

'And I miss you, Jerry!' she whispered back. 'Only a couple of days and I'll be home, we'll be home. Jerry, you're glad about Paul? About having another son, aren't you?'

He gave her his charming smile and patted her hand.

'Proud as Punch!' he said. 'Now I suppose I'd better push off or I shall have Sister telling me I'm tiring you. You still look rather pale, Lynn. Sure you feel all right?'

'Just tired!' Lynn reassured him. 'You look tired, too, Jerry! Nervous exhaustion. Have an early night.'

A moment or two after Jerry had kissed her good-bye, the nurse came in to 'top and tail' Paul and give the baby to her to feed. He was crying lustily now and Lynn remembered again with relief the young nursery nurse who would be with them for a month after she got home. Having Paul had tired her more than the other two children seemed to have done, and she was glad to think that, for a while at least, Betty would be able to get up to feed the baby at night!

After Paul was fed and she herself had had supper, Philip's white flowers and the red roses Jerry had sent the evening before were taken from her room and by eight o'clock she was fast asleep. In his crib beside those of the other sleeping babies, young Paul slept, too.

149

At his home, his godfather sat by himself, pondering thoughtfully the question of a christening present for him and the problem of its being valuable without giving offence to his parents. And at home, Paul's father sat in an armchair holding a book but not reading it as he unobtrusively studied the girl who sat sewing quietly on the other side of the fire.

CHAPTER TEN

'Why don't the children call you Betty?'

The girl looked up from her sewing and smiled uncertainly.

'Well, I suppose they prefer their own nickname, Mr. Birch.'

Jerry stood up and walked across to the table to pour himself a drink.

'Would you like one?' he asked. She shook her head.

'I don't think so . . . well, all right, I will. Thank you very much.'

He poured out the drinks and handed one to her. For a brief second their eyes met and then the girl bent her head quickly and put the glass down beside her.

'Well, what *do* they call you?' Jerry asked as he went back to his own chair with a smile at the corner of his mouth. (So she was not entirely unaware of him after all!)

'You . . . you'll laugh, I'm afraid. They call me Barbie!'

'Whatever for?' Jerry said.

She looked at him steadily for a moment.

'They seem to think I resemble Sue's Barbie doll. It's just their nonsense!'

Jerry laughed . . . an intimate laugh that forced the girl's eyes back to her sewing. Far from being unaware of her employer, she was all too painfully aware of his attraction. When their eyes had met for the first time, the evening she had arrived at this house, she had felt that tiny betraying trembling of her nerves and had known that here was a potential danger. She had wondered if after all she had been wise to stay on that first meeting, for she had known before what it meant to be violently attracted to a man. It was three years now since that other affair had ended and she had imagined herself immune to anyone but the young medical student who could not afford to marry her. But the moment she saw Jerry . . . so unmistakably male and handsome, a provocative challenge in those dark eyes, she had known herself succumbing for the second time in her life to a deep sexual attraction.

But after the first week in this house she found every possible reason for staying. She firmly believed that she had been mistaken in thinking Jerry Birch had given her that 'special' look and that he was the most devoted and affectionate of husbands. Moreover, she liked his wife, and the two children, and she was being paid an excellent salary. It was the kind of job she liked, too, for it was only a two-month appointment and above all she liked variety and constant change. So she had forgotten her first strange instinct to get away. Even if her body could not entirely forget the presence of Jerry Birch when he came into the room or passed her in the corridor, she refused to contemplate its implications or recognize the plain truth that she was as much attracted to him as she had ever been to Bill.

She thought now of Bill almost with surprise. She had fallen desperately in love with him. As a student he was terribly hard up, and had years of study still ahead of him. There was no hope of his marrying. She had tried to force the issue by giving him an ultimatum, for she knew she was not willing to wait indefinitely. His career had won. He had ended their affair on the grounds that it would not be fair to keep her tied.

She had been too proud to go back to him and tell him she would after all prefer to wait for him. And deep in her heart, she knew that now she was free again, she was not likely to remain faithful to him for long. But until now, she had not met another man who so appealed to her senses, and even while she was glad to feel that wild exhilaration once again and to know herself 'over' Bill, she was afraid. This man was already married and no good could come of a relationship between them. She had certain moral standards and making love to another woman's husband while she was away having his child was very much against her principles. Nevertheless, she could not still that trembling of her nerves when he was near her, and for the last twenty-four hours she had been all too fully aware of a distinct change in Jerry Birch's attitude to her!

It had started the evening before when he had asked her to eat with him.

'There's really no need for you to eat with the children. Tell Mary to lay your place in here and that I requested it!'

It meant no extra work for Mary and his suggestion had seemed reasonable. But was there another reason? She had found herself wondering . . . and tried at the same time not to be hoping there might be.

Jerry's behaviour and manners had been above reproach and there had been nothing more than the most casual of conversations between them. Yet still she sensed danger and she had gone to her own room as soon as the meal was over. Later she heard Jerry Birch go out.

This evening he had again asked her to join him at supper and afterwards suggested that she should watch a film on the T.V. in the living-room with him. But there had been no film and they had been sitting quietly, she with her sewing, he with a newspaper, until this moment.

'I'm trying to remember which of Sue's many dolls she calls "Barbie"!' he was saying.

'I think I would rather you didn't identify her!'

'If it's that long-legged glamorous blond, then I think it suits you beautifully! May I ask how old you are?'

'Didn't Mrs. Birch tell you? I'm twenty-two.'

'Boyfriend? I can't believe you're completely unattached.'

She felt the colour steal into her cheeks at the implied compliment and because she felt nervous of the personal turn the conversation had taken.

'No. I have no boyfriend, Mr Birch. I was engaged once but we broke it off . . . by mutual consent.'

'I see. Do you really have to call me "Mr Birch"? I can see no reason to be so formal. Surely "Jerry" will do?'

For the first time, the girl felt a real tremor of fear. Suppose her employer were not just an attractive man looking for a harmless flirtation? Suppose he were really a dangerous person? Suppose he was one of those men who were charming to their wives but murdered other women from some perverted motive like Nielson? Or like Lord Lucan who supposedly killed his children's nanny! Mary went home after she washed the supper things and she would then be quite alone in the house with this man. Suppose he attacked her?

She looked up startled as he gave a sudden laugh.

'My dear girl, don't look so terrified. Do you think I intend to eat you? You look scared out of your wits!'

She relaxed a little and gave him a half-smile. How stupid and gauche and imaginative she was being! Nothing could possibly happen which she herself did not wish to happen. This man was hardly a maniac! He was a civilized person like herself. Then why did she feel afraid of him? Unsure of herself?

'Perhaps I am a little afraid.' The words came out in a rush quite uncontrolled and she wished them back immediately.

'Of me? You have no need to be. I'm a model husband these days!'

She looked at him enquiringly.

'I don't quite understand . . .'

'My dear girl, how could you? I'm talking in riddles I dare say. I suppose you would be shocked if I told you I thought you were very attractive?'

She bit her lip nervously.

'I'm not shocked!'

'Surprised?'

'Perhaps, a little. I think I'd better go upstairs now.' Jerry laughed again, suddenly startling her.

'Don't do that! I'll behave, I promise. Betty, you're not a child. You must know how attractive you are. You can't exactly blame me for saying so, can you?'

She felt her heart leap and hurriedly fought down the queer tightness in her throat.

'I don't think you ought to be saying so!'

'I suppose not! I suppose the *right* thing to do is to go on pretending that you aren't here at all.' He walked past her and stood looking out of the window into the shadows in the garden. 'Heaven knows I've tried to do that, ever since you came here. But it isn't exactly easy, you know.'

I really must go now, before he says anything more, the girl thought. But she could not move. Every instinct longed to hear more and she could not go . . . not just yet.

He turned round and looked at her across the width of the room; but it was as if he had touched her and again the colour flared into her cheeks.

'Haven't you felt anything . . . anything at all?'

'No!' she said quickly, loudly; too quickly.

He smiled.

'You don't lie very well. Strange how these things happen. It's there or it isn't there.'

She knew what he meant . . . that unaccountable sexual attraction. It knew no barriers. Yet there was a barrier—an insurmountable barrier between them.

'You're married.' She all but whispered the words.

156

He turned his head in a curious angry gesture.

'Oh, yes, remind me of that. And because I am married I must lead a totally unnatural life; be a paragon of all the virtues and have no faults. But I'm not inhuman, Betty. Can *you* understand that? Man is not proof against his emotions. It would be a lie to pretend for a moment that there was not something about you . . . something that I have been trying hopelessly to fight against. You have felt it, too.'

She would not admit or deny it, yet her silence was all the admission he needed. A moment later he was beside her and had pulled her roughly into his arms.

'Let me go! Please let me go!' she cried, but her voice weakened with her senses and his lips came down on hers.

She was trembling violently when he released her and her whole body felt bruised and ached with unsatisfied longing. Watching him walk away from her, she marvelled at his calmness.

'I suppose I ought not to have done that!'

'Don't you love your wife?' she asked. He turned round with that quick gesture she was beginning to know was characteristic of him.

'Love her? Yes, I suppose so. But one can love so many different people so many different ways. What is love, Betty? Can you answer me? Can you tell me the difference

157

between love and passion? Is it part of sexual attraction? Whatever it is I want you desperately. I want to make love to you.'

And I want you to, she thought, but did not speak the words.

'I don't know what love is!' she said weakly. 'I don't know!'

'Betty!'

He was touching her now, his hands on her hips, his eyes looking deep down into hers, turning her thoughts into a mad whirlwind.

'Betty, you belong to me. Say you belong to me. You know that!'

'Yes! Yes!' Her hands went to his head and she brought his mouth fiercely back to her own. This was madness; this was bad, wrong; this was something she had never dreamed of—beauty that blinded; feelings that were too ecstatic to be denied.

'Jerry, Jerry . . .!'

Triumphantly he smiled, knowing that victory was soon to be his. But he knew better than to press his advantage for he knew that women wanted more from sex than just sex. He could wait. Tenderly he touched her cheek, her lips, her breast and felt her heart throb beneath his hand.

CHAPTER ELEVEN

'I do believe he's enjoying this, too!' Marion said, poking a finger in Paul's carry-cot. Now a month old, baby Paul had lost his first crumpled redness and was a beautiful child with a soft fuzz of fair hair and bright china-blue eyes. Like all babies the white of his eyes was blue, too, and Philip could not stop exclaiming the fact. He adored the child; 'doted' on him, Marion said, and made every possible excuse to hold him and admire him.

Lynn laughed happily. She felt so young and well and this day, in particular, was proving such fun! Philip had surprised them all by suggesting a picnic in his old home with Marion and Jack and the children. The weather had been sunny and warm for days and showed no sign of changing and he told them—truthfully they had discovered for themselves—that there were few places in England prettier than his home in May.

So they had driven down together this morning and, to the older children's unutterable delight, lit a big fire in the great inglenook fireplace and fried sausages and chips over it. Nothing had tasted quite so good for ages!

Lynn had wondered if perhaps nostalgia for days that were gone would make Philip morose and quiet, but far from it, he had been the life and soul of the party, teasing David and Sue, chaffing Jack, talking and explaining places and things to Marion and Lynn. He seemed to have dropped ten years from his age, and because of his enormous enjoyment they were all having a wonderful time.

It was true, thought Lynn as she drank her coffee, that there could be no place more beautiful than Philip's home in May. In spite of the house being empty, unfurnished and faintly damp, as unlived-in houses generally are, this one seemed to soak up the sunshine and throw back an atmosphere of warmth and happiness. Maybe it was just reflecting Philip's carefree mood. Whatever it was, there was nothing of the chill of abandonment about it. The walls and rooms seemed almost to be welcoming them as the children ran in and out of them laughing and shouting as they made discoveries.

It was a rambling old Elizabethan farmhouse with at least fourteen rooms. The kitchen was enormous, with a giant range and big built-in dresser that must at one time, Lynn imagined, have been hung with old Wedgwood blue and white china. No wonder Philip's childhood had been so happy there. He and Jack had reminisced in a spontaneous happy way that had shown both of them in a new light to Marion and Lynn watching them.

'I say, Pip, this was Martin's room.

Remember the night we climbed down the creeper and had a midnight rendezvous in the graveyard? None of us admitted it but we were scared stiff. Look, there's one of the tin soldiers. It must have rolled under there years ago! Look, David, we used to have a whole army of these and we had battles galore! More often than not they developed into personal battles between ourselves!'

'It's a shame no one lives here now!' Philip said, more to himself than to the others, when they finished their tour of the rooms and were lighting the fire on which to fry their lunch. For a moment they had all fallen silent and nostalgia had threatened them. Then David and Sue had come into the room shouting that they had discovered a swing in the garden and the sadness passed.

'I've eaten too much!' said Jack, finishing off his beer none the less. 'This is fun, Pip. Whatever made you think of it?'

Philip lit his pipe and shrugged his shoulders at the same time.

'Don't know, really. Perhaps I always do think of the old place at this time of year. Then suddenly the idea came to me . . . why not go and see it; take Lynn and the children, too, and have a picnic? We'll go and see the garden afterwards, shall we?'

'Yes, let's!' Lynn agreed eagerly. 'I'll feed Paul in a moment and then he can nap before we go home.'

'I'll take you up to Mother's room. It's always so sunny and warm in there,' Philip said easily.

Lynn walked over and took the baby out of his cot and held him close to her. He was so amazingly good that she could hardly believe how little trouble he had been. She had to be at least half an hour late for his feed for him to begin to announce his hunger in a lusty yell. But mostly he just slept or lay with his eyes open, yawning sometimes. He was the most contented baby she had known. Perhaps it was because she herself was feeding him and was herself so contented. The perfection of her life had never varied once from that moment in the nursing-home when he was born. Only the very faintest of worries had assailed her and that was when Betty had given notice the week after she got home. The girl had given no reason except that she had been offered another job which she would lose if she did not go immediately.

Lynn had tried somewhat angrily to point out the predicament she would be in and how unfair it was to walk out on her side of the agreement. But oddly enough the girl had been completely adamant and had had the nerve to say (quite truthfully as it had turned out): 'Surely Mary can manage! Paul is so good that he's no trouble and David starts school again next week, doesn't he? I don't see that I'm really of any use at all.'

It was true! Paul seldom disturbed them at night and David and Sue were behaving beautifully and causing her no bother. Mary was in any case doing all the cooking and cleaning, and had offered to stay on later to do any ironing or mending. So it turned out that they had been paying Betty a salary and keeping her when they could manage very well without her. And Lynn was glad now that she had gone and she had Jerry and the children to herself again.

She followed Philip upstairs to the room. Philip and Jack by some tacit understanding had omitted to take them into it this morning. It led off one of the larger bedrooms and strangely none of them had noticed the door earlier.

A wave of sunshine seemed to sweep over them as they went in. Lynn gave a little cry of delight as she looked round and saw the charming old window seat beneath the leaded-light casement windows.

'It's beautiful!' she told Philip. 'I'd love to live here!' Philip walked away and stood looking out into the garden. He ignored her remark and said slowly:

'I'll leave you alone to feed that young man now.'

Without realizing what made her act so spontaneously, Lynn unbuttoned her dress and put the baby to her breast.

'Don't go unless you want to, Philip. I don't

163

mind your being here and it's nice to have someone to talk to.'

He turned slowly and sat down on the window seat opposite to the side where Lynn was seated with the baby. His hands were twisting his unlit pipe as if he were unwilling to look at her. But presently he did look up and found her fair head bent over the baby's tiny one. His eyes were suddenly full of pain and even while he marvelled at the sight of the woman he loved so dearly feeding her child, he wished she had not asked him to stay. It showed so clearly how completely without feeling she was for him. Oh, not without any feeling. He knew that she regarded him as a very dear friend . . . almost as a brother! But that was not the way he wanted her to feel about him even while he knew it was the only way if he was not to lose her altogether!

She looked up and, seeing his eyes on her, smiled.

'He's terribly greedy, isn't he?'

Philip said gruffly:

'I expect Jerry's very proud of him.'

Lynn laughed.

'Oh, yes, I think he is. But he's not really very fond of babies—at least, not very new ones. He likes them best when they first start to say "Da-da" and recognize him.'

'You're very happy now, Lynn? No, I've no *need* to ask you that. It shines out of your eyes.'

Lynn moved the baby over to her other

164

breast and said sincerely:

'Life's just perfect, Philip. I get the feeling every now and again that it's too good to last. Still no news of Marcia?'

'No, none! I told you, didn't I, that I traced her to a hotel in Devon? But she didn't leave a forwarding address after that and I don't see how we can find out any more without asking her uncle or somebody. I thought maybe she might return to her flat in that mews eventually. It was only let for a year, you know. Maybe she intends to come back when it's all over.'

'Yes. That's possible. We'll wait till the year is up next month and then you could call at the flat again, Philip. I know it's stupid of me but I can't help wondering all the time what has happened to her. I wouldn't worry if I knew for sure she was over it all and the baby was in good hands. I wish I could have asked Jerry where she was.'

'But surely *he* doesn't know?'

Lynn smiled at the horror in Philips voice.

'No, of course not! But he could so easily mention her name casually to Henderson, his boss. But I can't bring myself to tell Jerry I remember her. I'm sure he thinks I've forgotten all about her and I really believe Jerry, himself, never thinks of her. It was just a passing phase, Philip, which meant nothing at all to him. That's one of the reasons I felt so sorry for her. She was obviously in love with

165

him

'I suppose he *is* very attractive to women.'

'Well, yes,' Lynn agreed, 'but that doesn't exactly excuse him going off the rails, Philip. But don't let's talk about that. It's all over now and I know he'd never do anything like that again. We're so happy now . . . happier than we've ever been.'

'I'm glad!' Philip said, truthfully, too. The most important thing in the world to him was her happiness. So long as that lasted he was content to stay in the background of her life. But underneath the surface of that contentment lay an iron resolve . . let Jerry Birch hurt his wife once more and he, Philip, would be there to protect her!

Quite what he would do he had not yet fathomed, but he was far too deeply in love with Lynn to sit back a second time while he saw her let down by a man even less worthy of her than himself! His own private opinion of Birch was that he cashed in on his attraction for the opposite sex and seemed without any moral standards at all. He, Philip, had heard about this man's behaviour with his first wife before he knew that Lynn was his second wife! And he believed, now he had met Jerry, every word Hedges had said about him. He believed that Jane had been let down just as Lynn had been; and that in the end Jane had been able to take no more of it.

Would there be any more for Lynn to take?

He sincerely hoped for her sake that she was justified in her belief in the future. He knew better than most just how deeply she cared about her husband; just how desperately she had been hurt by his unfaithfulness. But he was convinced that she had no real idea as to the kind of man she had married. She believed in him; made every excuse for him because she was blinded by her love for him. It was a very shaky foundation on which to base her life's happiness.

If only I had met her years ago . . . before she married him! he thought, not for the first but for the hundredth time. And back came the inevitable reply from his heart: Lynn would not have married him, Philip, even had she been free. She felt nothing for him other than friendly affection. He was not attractive to women as was Jerry Birch. He knew from his own reflection in the mirror that he had none of the recognized good looks that a woman as beautiful as Lynn might expect as her right.

In this viewpoint, Philip was strangely immature. He had not yet realized that women do not necessarily love a physical image but the man behind it. Jack, for instance, was not much better to look at than he was and yet Marion thought him the most attractive husband any girl could have. She loved him. But then, Philip told himself, Marion was not Lynn. Dear, plump, friendly Marion was far from being a 'beauty' even while her smiling, contented, round little face had great charm.

Yet I could have made Lynn happy! Philip thought not without bitterness even while he was without conceit. I would have cared for her with all the love in the world. I would have protected her and lived only for her and the children. (He forgot for the moment that David and Sue and Paul were not his children, too!) I could afford to keep them all in a reasonable standard of luxury. We could have lived here in this house; perhaps had more children to keep us happy in our old age . . .

'A penny for your thoughts, Philip!'

He gathered them together quickly and with a rather forced smile, said:

'Castles in Spain, Lynn. They wouldn't interest you.'

'But they would, Philip. You know how interested I am in you and your life.'

She started to pat the baby's back with an absorbed attention that somehow made him think of a little girl playing with her doll and lost to the outside world. If only that world could be prevented from hurting her! If only she could keep her innocence!

'My dear, my life is very dull and the only real interest in it is you and your family. I'm lucky, aren't I, to have you all . . . a ready-made family with none of its responsibilities.' Lynn laughed, not taking him seriously.

'I'm quite certain you never evaded a responsibility in your life, Philip, or wanted to. So I refuse to allow you to make yourself out to be taking everything and giving nothing back. On the contrary, in fact, I feel that it is I and the children who take everything and give nothing.'

'Mutual congratulation society!' Philip said flippantly to cover his real feelings. How adept he was becoming at that trick! 'Now if you've finished with my young godson for the moment, let's go out to the garden before the sun loses its warmth.'

It was wild and overgrown now but Lynn could see beneath the twisting bindweed and tall grasses to what it had once been. The lavender hedge that bounded the sandstone terrace was badly in need of clipping but already the steady hum of bees about the tight buds gave promise of the beautiful scent that would come from them when the buds opened. Beyond, the cherry, apple, almond and plum trees were a mass of snow-white and rose-pink blossom. The ground sloped gently away and then flattened out abruptly.

'That was the tennis court!' Philip explained. 'We dug, levelled and sowed the grass ourselves and Father gave us a net and racquets as a reward for our labours. We had some wonderful parties and even had dreams of Wimbledon. Derek and Martin were specially good . . .'

'Uncle Philip, what's this funny wooden thing? Down in the long grass?' David cried

169

excitedly.

'That's an old well,' Philip explained, bending down and pulling the grass and weeds away. 'It was never used as it was so far from the house . . . or at least, not in our lifetime. There's spring water down there. As a matter of fact, we did talk once of digging ourselves a lake but we found out it was forty feet or so below ground level and decided it was too much to tackle! Goodness, Jack, remember the time Jim fell down there and we had to fish him out in the bucket?'

'Was he very frightened, Uncle Philip?'

'Well, no, oddly enough. He'd found an old toad on the way up and he was more concerned about staking his claim to it than the fact that he was dripping wet . . . and well water is pretty cold, I can tell you!'

'I wish we lived here!' David cried, jumping up and down. 'Can't we live here, Mummy?'

Lynn shook her head.

'It's Uncle Philip's house, my poppet. And even if he agreed to rent it to us, it would be too far away for Daddy to get up and down to London each day.'

'Never mind him!' David cried, forgetting himself in his enthusiasm that contained all a child's concentration for the desire of the moment. 'He could come here at weekends!'

Lynn checked him quickly and at the same time felt a little nagging shaft of pain in her heart. David couldn't really mean it, of course, but it did hurt her a little to think that Jerry's son could write him off, however thoughtlessly, as a matter of no consequence. David was growing up, of course, and he was emotionally a lot more independent than he had been. It was right and natural that he should make friends at school and develop interests outside his home and family. All the same, he had so adored Jerry once. Must growing up necessarily entail loss of affection for one's parents? Did he feel that same way about her, his mother? She longed to question him and yet could not bring herself to do so. Walking back to the house, David suddenly clung to her arm and, slowing her pace to his, they fell behind the others.

'I didn't really mean that about Daddy!' he said suddenly. Had he then been so sensitive to her reactions that even at the tender age of seven he had realized his words had hurt her?

'Of course, darling, I knew that!' she said as calmly as she could.

'All the same, it would be nice, wouldn't it? I mean, you'd be here and Sue and Paul and Mary and Uncle Philip. I mean, we'd be really too busy in this house and garden to miss him, wouldn't we? And it would be nice for him, too, at week-ends.'

'David!' Her voice was sharp and he turned his head round to hers, gazing at her with the complete innocence and candour of a child. Did he not realize what he had implied? No,

171

she thought, he just spoke from his heart.

'David, don't you love Daddy?'

'Oh, yes, of course I do!' David said, relieved that he could speak quite openly. For one moment he had thought his mother was going to be cross!

'But if you love people, you want them to be near you! Why, we should all be dreadfully lonely without Daddy here in the evenings.'

'Well, we'd have Uncle Philip, wouldn't we?'

Lynn wished she had not started this conversation. But she could not terminate it quite yet.

'No, David, we wouldn't. Uncle Philip couldn't live in this house with us.'

'Why not?'

'Well, because I'm not married to him. Only married people or relations live together in one house as one family.'

'But what about Barbie? She isn't a relation, is she? She lived with us.'

'Yes, darling, but she was different. We engaged her to work for us just as we do Mary.'

'But I still don't see why Uncle Philip couldn't live with us. I mean, he could work for us, too, couldn't he? He's got nobody else to work for, has he? And he is kind of related to Paul, isn't he?'

Lynn sighed. How difficult it was explaining the conventions to a child of David's age!

172

Children were so literal, and the way they saw things, the clean, pure way, made explanations impossible.

'Daddy wouldn't like it,' she said at last. 'And nor would I. We like to be by ourselves . . . just our own family circle. That's the way it's supposed to be . . . Mummy and Daddy and the children.'

'But I'd *like* Uncle Philip to live with us!' David persisted.

I suppose I ought not to be jealous on Jerry's account! Lynn told herself reasonably. All small boys have these hero-worshipping phases. And Philip's been so good with him. If only Jerry gave him a little more time and attention!

'I know, Mummy, we'll live here with Uncle Philip in the holidays and we'll go back to Daddy for term-time.'

Half-irritated, half-amused, Lynn said:

'But who'd look after Daddy while we were away?'

'Well, Barbie could, couldn't she? Like she did when you were in the nursing-home? Daddy likes her, so that would be all right! You could ask her to come back.'

Finish this conversation now, some inner instinct told Lynn. Keep your faith! Trust Jerry! That was a perfectly innocent remark. We all liked Betty. I won't question my own son about his father. I won't say a word . . .

'We all liked Betty, darling, but that doesn't

173

mean Daddy would like her to look after him for long. Besides he loves you and me and Sue and Paul and he wants to be with us.'

'Well, he wants to be with her, too, so why can't we all live together always?'

No, no, no! a little voice screamed in Lynn's ear, or was it in her heart? I won't let this conversation continue. 'You're talking rubbish, David. And the whole thing is quite out of the question in any case, so let's say no more about it. Now run along and find Sue and the others.'

David looked at her in surprise. She seldom used that 'shutting-up' tone of voice to him; never in fact, unless he had done something very bad. It wasn't fair. He hadn't done anything wrong now! He felt the need to justify himself and risking her further displeasure at his disobedience, he said:

'But it isn't rubbish, Mummy. He does like her. That's why she went away. I heard her say so, so there!'

So it was out now. She had tried to prevent it, but not knowing what it was she'd had to prevent, she had failed.

'When? Please explain what you mean, David!'

Her voice was quiet . . . too quiet, but the child had never been afraid of speaking out to his mother so long as he was speaking the truth. He said:

'Why, when you were away, Mummy. It was the night Sue wet her bed . . . well, she said she hadn't but she *was* wet and so was her nightie so I 'spect she did it in her sleep!'

'Nobody told me!' Lynn said, biting her lip. 'Go on, David!'

'She was crying and woke me up so I thought I'd better go and tell Barbie but she wasn't in her bedroom so I went downstairs and she was in there with Daddy.'

'In where?'

'In the living-room. I heard them talking and Daddy said, 'You do love me, don't you?' and she said: 'Yes, that's why I must go away. It isn't fair to her.' I don't see why it isn't fair, and Mummy, who's "her"? At any rate I went in and then Barbie came out and I think she'd been crying 'cos her eyes looked funny. Next day she said I wasn't to tell you anything about Sue wetting her bed or coming to find her or anything because you might be worried about it and it wasn't fair to worry you when you weren't very strong. She said mothers weren't strong after they'd had babies and that's why they have to stay in bed. But you're strong now, aren't you, Mummy? It's all right to tell you?'

'Yes, David!'

'You're not cross, Mummy? About Sue, I mean? There's a boy at school who wets his bed and his Mummy is dreadfully cross but I don't think that's fair, do you? You can't help it if you do it in your sleep, can you?'

'No, dearest, and I'm not at all cross with

175

Sue. Now run along, darling, and see if you can find the others. It's time we went home.'

He seemed quite happy now he had proved his point and he ran off skipping happily, unaware of the devastation he had left behind him; the utter and complete devastation of a woman's life, her world, her heart.

'You're strong now, aren't you, Mummy?'

Yes, she was strong now . . . strong enough to do the only thing left for her to do. This time she would not be so weak. Jerry had had his chance and he had lost it. She could not find it in her heart to forgive him again.

She sat down weakly on an old bench beneath one of the blossoming apple trees, feeling faint with physical weakness. Her hands began to tremble and she felt ice-cold.

Shock! she thought, but it was automatic and she made no move to go after her son.

Philip found her there and said:

'My dear, you look awful! Are you ill? Why, you're shivering! I ought not to have brought you. It's been too much for you so soon after Paul.'

'Philip, I want to go home!'

'But of course! You're not well. I'll call Marion right away. We can get you a brandy on the way. Here, take my arm.'

She allowed him to help her up and walked with him back to the house. Now the sunlight and the beauty mocked her and her children's happy laughter was like a knife piercing her heart.

This time it never for a second occurred to her to doubt the inference of David's words or to draw the worst conclusions as to what had happened. She felt, strangely, that she was almost prepared . . . not for the first shock of hearing . . . but for the greater pain of believing. It was as if she had in her heart been waiting all the time for this to happen. But knowing did not make it any easier to bear.

CHAPTER TWELVE

'I swear you're on the wrong track, Lynn. Great Heavens, you must believe me!'

'And accuse David, who hasn't lied to me for years, of making up such a fantastic story for no reason at all?'

She faced him across the room, bitterness in her eyes, her voice hard. He spread out his hands in a gesture that said: 'You're being quite unreasonable but I deserve it. Nevertheless I'll prove you're misjudging me.' His calmness was beginning to disconcert her.

'My dear Lynn, don't be silly! Of course David wouldn't make up a story like that; he's far too young to know what he's talking about. I'm only saying that he got mixed up. Great Scott, Lynn, it's over a month since the girl was in the house. David can't be expected

177

to remember word for word something that couldn't have meant very much to him anyway!'

'Well, what are you suggesting he did hear?'

Jerry calmly lit a cigarette and sat down in the armchair. Then he said:

'I'm suggesting he heard part of the truth. But he got mixed up as to who was talking. What actually transpired was this: Betty had told me that she wanted to give in her notice. I asked her why and she refused to say. Not having a clue as to the real reason, I pressed her for a reason, saying it was very awkward and unfair to you to go off like that without saying. And then she said she had fallen in love with me! Naturally, I was pretty surprised. Apart from dinner-table conversation, we'd barely exchanged more than a few words.'

He got up and went across to the corner cupboard and poured himself a drink. Lynn's eyes followed his every move but she did not speak.

'So I told her not to be so silly, and frankly, I didn't believe her. Then she burst into tears and said: "I do love you, that's why I must go away. It wouldn't be fair to her." Then David came in. I didn't see her again that evening, but next morning at breakfast I told her I would accept a week's notice, and she asked me not to tell you what she had said and I promised I wouldn't. It was to save you worry, Lynn.'

His tone became suddenly arrogant.

'Don't think that I've ever for one moment believed you trusted me! I knew the kind of conclusions you would jump to if I told you the truth. It's really your fault, Lynn. If you were a little less suspicious, this wouldn't have happened. You don't believe me now, do you?'

'I don't know what to believe,' Lynn said weakly. 'I just don't know, Jerry!'

'Oh, but you're more than ready to think the worst!' Jerry's voice was bitter. 'I suppose I deserve that because of what happened in the past. But I had hoped that you were going to allow me to forget the past. For how long must a man go on paying for past sins?'

It seemed now as if she were the one on the defensive. Surely Jerry could not be so calm, so reasonable, if he were really guilty! Had she in fact misjudged him? *If only she knew what to believe!*

'I'm trying not to remember the past, Jerry. I don't want to be unfair but you must admit that it's all against you, on the surface, anyway. You yourself admit that *she* was in love with *you*. Do you really think a girl can fall in love and say so without any encouragement of any sort?'

'But why ever not? I don't for a moment believe Betty was really in love . . . of course not. She just thought she was. Look at it this way, Lynn, a young girl, unattached, on the rebound from some doctor fellow, who'd let

179

her down . . . it's not unreasonable that she should think she'd fallen for me. I dare say I probably smiled at her once or twice without realizing it. As a matter of fact, I rather liked her. She was telling me one evening about the jobs she'd been in and I was interested. She may have thought I was more than "just interested"; that I was showing a special kind of interest in her. But if I did that, it was perfectly innocent and I must say I feel pretty bitter about your condemnation when for once I am blameless!'

He's telling the truth! Lynn thought. He wouldn't lie so coolly. No man could. Probably he did flirt a little bit with her. He can't help making himself attractive to women. It's unconscious with him, like eating and drinking and breathing.

'And you haven't seen Betty since?'

Did he hesitate for the barest fraction of a second? Lynn, watching him, was not sure.

Then he said firmly:

'Of course not! When could I possibly have seen her and why should I have wanted to? Really, Lynn, life is getting pretty intolerable. Jealousy isn't easy to live with, you know.'

'Nor is mistrust!' Lynn said helplessly. 'What has happened to us, Jerry? I don't understand. Believe me, I'm not jealous . . . not of any mythical person; not just for the sake of being jealous. I don't mind your friendship with other women. I was jealous of

180

Marcia, but then so would any wife have been. It's just that somehow . . . well, I can't trust you, Jerry. It isn't a nice thing to say but it's true. I don't even feel certain now that you're telling me the truth.'

'Are you trying to tell me that you aren't in love with me any more?'

His words struck a strange icy chill in her heart.

'No, no, I'm not!' she said fiercely. 'Don't you see that it is because I love you, Jerry, that I cannot bear there to be anything wrong between us? I want everything to be perfect— always.'

He came towards her and put his hands on her shoulders, looking deep into her troubled eyes with an unfathomable expression in his own.

'But nothing is ever perfect, my dear, and least of all is perfection to be found in human relationships.'

She heard her voice tremble as she questioned him helplessly:

'Hasn't our marriage ever seemed perfect to you, Jerry?'

His hands dropped to his sides and he walked away from her to pick up his half-empty glass.

'Of course it has, Sweetheart. But we've had our bad moments just as other people have had theirs. Unfortunately I let you down and that seemed to shake your faith in me not just for a little while, but for always. Now, I can't make the smallest gesture of friendship towards another woman but you accuse me of being unfaithful. It isn't a very happy position to find myself in, is it?'

Lynn bit her lip. What reply could she give him but to acknowledge her own guilt? She hadn't ever really trusted him; not blindly! She had been over-ready to believe the worst at the slightest suspicion, and she had condemned him all too easily this last time without giving him the chance to make his explanation. Whatever was wrong between them now was her doing.

Nevertheless deep down inside her, she could not feel either reassured or happy. What future had they together on such a footing? Could she herself change? Could she begin again to feel that same wonderful safeness and security in Jerry's love that had been so miraculously there when they were first married? Could she regain a state of mind?

She felt deeply depressed and unhappy; and an overwhelming longing for Jerry to say something to reassure and comfort her caused her to go to him and hold out her hands appealingly.

'Jerry, you do love me, don't you? Really love me?'

He took her hands and gave them a friendly little squeeze.

'But, my sweet, of course I do. You

shouldn't let yourself get worked up about things. You think too much; get yourself tied up in knots. Can't you ever learn to accept life as it is?'

'Life, yes!' Lynn cried passionately. 'But I can't learn to accept second best in love; in our marriage, Jerry.'

'Is it second best?'

She bit her lip again, afraid she had hurt him by that impulsive phrase, sprung from her lips.

'No. But I'm so afraid it might become that, Jerry. I think I've always been a little afraid that our marriage wasn't quite so important to you as it is to me; that I'm only part of your life whereas you are all of mine!'

He shrugged his shoulders in a gesture of helplessness.

'You're so intense, Lynn! Take it easy, Poppet, and don't get so het up over nothing. What you say is true only in so far as most men have interests outside their home . . . their work and men friends and so on. And it isn't true to say that I am "all your life". You have the children and I have to share you with them. It isn't a good thing to be too possessive.'

'And you think I'm too possessive?'

He gave her his charming smile that took the sting out of his words of assent.

'But no worse than most women, I dare say! Come, Sweetheart, let's have a smile. I've tried so hard to make you happy and it isn't easy for me to see how badly I've failed.'

She was in his arms then, filled with remorse and resolution.

'Forgive me, Jerry! I know I've been beastly . . . doubting you. I'll be different, I promise. It's just that I love you so desperately that I can't bear even the thought of your caring for any other woman.'

'Green eyes!' Jerry murmured as he bent his head to touch her lips. 'Blue, really . . . beautiful eyes!'

What power he has over me, Lynn marvelled as her heart quickened its beat when he kissed her. I belong to him. Life would be meaningless without him. Jerry, Jerry . . .

Looking down at those eyes, closed now, at the faint flush on her cheeks, at the softly parted lips so close to his own, Jerry gave a smile of satisfaction. This woman was his to manipulate as he wished. Here was his one great triumph . . . his lasting pride. Here in his arms was the ultimate test of his power to have life the way *he* wanted it. Her constant love fed his insatiable vanity and gave him power. Only the beauty of her face and body could rob him of the smallest portion of it for that beauty could stir him to the weakness of desire. After seven years, he still felt his pulses quicken with the same sweet delight that with other women died so quickly after he had succeeded in seducing them. She alone had been able to keep him; to bring him back again and again to

184

her body. He had married her because of her physical attraction for him and because he had known that he must have her not just once but whenever he needed her. He, who had sworn never to be tied again, had been weakened by his own desires and by this strength in her! Well, he must pay the price of marriage from time to time. He had done so; he'd given her children, a home, his companionship. His side of the bargain was more than paid. And in return, she offered him herself . . . too much love, but never too much loving.

'Darling, darling Lynn!' he whispered. 'It's been such a long time. Surely now . . .'

'Yes!' she whispered back although they were quite alone. 'Yes, darling, now!'

She forgot that her doctor had advised her not to resume her physical relationship with her husband until at least two months after Paul's birth. Her body was a better judge and she longed now to give herself, heart and soul, to Jerry. Her eyes were filled with a deep love and tenderness as she opened her arms to him. Blinded by it, she did not see the triumphant little smile in Jerry's eyes as he claimed his payment for the freedom he had to forgo; for the tiresome little evasions, lies and subterfuges that *she* forced from him when he wanted a woman other than his wife.

*　　　*　　　*

'Philip! How glad I am to see you! I didn't realize until you phoned how anxious I've been for news.'

He looked down at Lynn's flushed face with surprise and a deep regret. His surprise was at the emotional intensity that she now and again revealed to him, but which for the most part lay concealed beneath her cool, fair, almost cold beauty. One expected fire and passion in the dark, colourful Spanish and Italian type of woman; a coldness in tall, graceful golden beauty such as Lynn's. But how wrong it was to judge character on appearance! Lynn's warmth and ardour stirred him to a new channel of love for her. It was not now just a matter of admiration or respect he felt; a desire to cherish and protect. It was more than that; became more each time he saw her and knew her better. Now he desired her as he had never before desired a woman, and his own protective armour of friendliness was difficult to maintain when he held her hand for a brief moment and felt his whole body tremble in recognition of her.

He had managed at last to obtain news of Marcia; news he feared would not be at all welcome but which he had to impart. He had telephoned Lynn and made this appointment to meet her at his Club. They sat now in the lounge waiting for the drinks he had ordered although she told him she ought not to be drinking any alcohol since she was still feeding

Paul. Maybe she felt she needed bracing for his news. Could it be she was afraid to hear what he had to tell her? Yet Marcia Henderson was not her responsibility.

'She had her baby in a hospital in Exeter six weeks ago. She is back at her flat now and is expecting to get married shortly. She told me this only when I explained that you had sent me and that your husband knew nothing whatever about our efforts to trace her.'

'That's a great relief!' Lynn said, her tension easing slowly. 'I'm glad she's getting married. Did she seem fairly happy, Philip?'

He bit his lip. This was the part he was afraid she might not like.

'Well, no, Lynn. I can't say she did. She . . . broke down at one point. When she calmed down a bit, I asked her if there was anything I could do. She told me there was one thing . . . to try to keep you from making any more enquiries about her or the baby. She seemed . . . frightened!'

'But why? She knows I would never tell a soul. As to her marriage, I told her myself I hoped that one day she might meet someone else. Philip, what else did she say?'

'Very little. I got the impression she was trying to hide something from me, Lynn. Of course, I may be wrong. Naturally she would be reticent with me, a complete stranger. In fact I was surprised she didn't just bang the door in my face. But as soon as I mentioned *your* name, she took me upstairs to her sitting-room.'

'You didn't see the . . . the baby?'

'No. I'm sure it wasn't in the flat. I've seen enough of the paraphernalia that goes with young Paul . . . nappies, powder, cream, etc., etc., to know what a baby in the house means! I did ask her if it was all right and she said "Yes", just like that, and changed the conversation.'

Lynn gave a deep sigh.

'I don't want to interfere in her life, Philip, especially as she has asked me through you not to do so. But I can't help feeling worried. Why should she break down like that? I could understand it if she were quite alone, but now she has met someone else. Philip, could it be something to do with the baby? She told me she intended to have it adopted so that would explain why there was no sign of it. But had she done so, why didn't she tell you it was in safe hands? Could it be ill? Have something wrong with it so it couldn't be placed for adoption? Perhaps it is with foster parents she doesn't like! I shan't be able to rest in peace until I know.'

Philip looked at her anxiously.

'Don't you think it might be better not to know, Lynn, my dear? It isn't your concern, your responsibility. Surely it would be better now you know she is all right just to forget all about her?'

'But Philip, that baby is a half brother or sister to Paul and to David and Sue! It's . . . Jerry's child!'

'By another woman!' Philip said with a harshness he had not intended but which slipped out unbidden. 'That should make you hate that child, Lynn.'

'But I don't . . . I couldn't!' Lynn whispered. 'I've lain awake at nights thinking about it, Philip. I've wondered what it looked like; thought again and again that it's almost Paul's twin! I've held Paul's tiny dimpled little hands in mine and found myself thinking: "Was it a girl, or a boy like him? Is someone holding that baby's hand? Is it good and sweet and cuddlesome like my baby? Is someone loving it as I love Paul?'

'Does Jerry know you feel like this?'

'No!' Lynn cried. 'You know I've never told him I met Marcia. Philip, would you do something for me? Something else I can't do for myself?'

'You know I'll do anything I can, Lynn.'

'Find out what has happened to that baby!'

'My dear, how can I? Do you want me to see Miss Henderson again? Or am I to play private detective and try and trace the child from Exeter?' His tone had been almost harsh and Lynn was looking at him in surprise.

'Philip, do you think it's wrong to do this?'

His face softened suddenly and became vulnerable in its sudden expression of

189

tenderness and love. But she was not looking at him with eyes which might see such emotions. She looked only for his opinion.

'No, not wrong! Unnecessary, perhaps. And I'm afraid for you, Lynn. I can't see how this knowledge will bring you any happiness or even peace of mind.'

She held his eyes for a moment with a question in her own and then he looked quickly away as she said:

'Philip, you know more than you've told me, don't you? You know more and don't want to tell me.'

He couldn't lie to her, yet he had hoped he need not reveal the unsavoury facts.

'Yes, I do know what has happened to the child. But I promised I wouldn't tell you. You can't ask me to break that promise.'

'Is it dead?' Lynn's voice was a whisper.

'No, it's alive and probably quite well. Please, my dear, don't torment yourself about it. Let sleeping dogs lie!'

'I can't!' Lynn said after a pause. 'Philip, at least tell me this much. Could you arrange to see the baby? You could, couldn't you? I can see in your face that it would be possible.'

'I suppose it's possible!' he agreed reluctantly.

'Then please, Philip, go and see it this afternoon. Let me know that it is being properly cared for and that it has some kind of future. Then I'll give you my word I won't ask you to do anything more. Please, Philip!'

He was not proof against her pleading. Her very wish to reassure herself about the child's welfare had only served to increase his love for her; his certainty that here was a really good woman; not good in its pious sense, but kind, selfless, altruistic; a woman with a truly maternal instinct who could not be at peace when she believed a child was ill or in need.

'Lynn, I love you very much!' Had he spoken those words aloud or only thought them? He saw her eyes widen, heard the sharp intake of her breath and knew he had in one moment relieved the great pressure on his heart by revealing the truth to her.

'Philip, I . . . I didn't know!'

He wanted to pretend that he hadn't really spoken those words or at least had meant them only in a friendly affection. But he could not lie about something which mattered so much to him.

'Forgive me; I ought not to have said that. I had no right to do so!'

He saw her hands clasp one another and her knuckles tighten; noticed inconsequently the bright gold of her fair head bent over those hands. Then she said:

'I think perhaps I've known it for a long time. I pretended to myself that it wasn't so. I was afraid of the truth.'

'Please, Lynn, try to forget that I said it. I couldn't bear to let you go out of my life completely. Your friendship is very very precious to me, my dear. Can you forget?'

Lynn was silent for a long moment. Then she raised her head and he saw with surprise that there was a smile behind the tears in her eyes.

'I don't really want to forget, Philip! I suppose that is very selfish of me but I'm so flattered that you should love me. I like and admire you so much, it has made me very proud to know that you . . . you feel that way. I'm only sorry because of *you*.'

'Don't be sorry for me, my dear. I'm perfectly happy knowing you value our friendship. I give you my word I won't speak of this again. I never meant to do so at all. But . . . well, there's no excuse. I simply couldn't help myself. Will you try and forget, or at least, not be sorry in the remembering? Don't let it make any difference between us.'

'No, of course not!' she said in a low, firm voice, and with a gesture that touched him deeply she held out her hand for him to take in his own.

'I . . . I expect it will wear off!' she said, just as she might have told David the pain of a cut finger would soon get better. He knew that it wasn't true; that probably she didn't believe it either, but she was trying to make things right between them and he let her speak. 'One of these days you'll meet a "brilliant" redhead . . . (she smiled as she used her son's favourite adjective) . . . and you'll wonder how you ever thought you liked me.'

'Loved you!' he could not refrain from correcting her.

Her face became suddenly very sad.

'Oh, Philip, why does everything in life have to be so complicated? Why must love always be thwarted, misused?'

'But, my dear, it is neither of those things. Sometimes it is unrequited but that is not "thwarted". It's still a good thing even when it is unsatisfied. Sometimes it is misplaced . . . but that does not lessen the merit of loving. Don't be sad!'

Lynn smiled a half-smile that covered her inner tears.

'You always know just the right thing to say, Philip. And you know so exactly what I am trying to say; what I mean.'

That's because I love you, he thought, but this time refrained from saying. Aloud he said:

'You love your husband, Lynn, and that is one example of love that is neither unrequited nor thwarted.'

This time it was Lynn who withheld the immediate thought, but it has been misused! Then she chided herself for doing just what she had promised Jerry not to do . . . harp on the past. They had begun a new phase of their life together and she trusted him now. She was once again confident of his love and of the rightness of their marriage.

Her thoughts swung swiftly back to the man at her side and for a brief second she was aware of a deep comfort from the large, strong hand that was holding her own. It gave her the same feeling of security that he always inspired in her. She knew that she was able to be herself with him and now, suddenly, she questioned her own behaviour. Had that satisfying feeling of being able to depend on him in some way transmitted itself to him and been a contributory factor to his falling in love with her? Had she taken too much from his proffered friendship and encouraged him to think that perhaps she felt more than just friendly towards him? But no, this was unlikely since she had never wanted more from him. He must know that she had never at any time come near to loving him; that she was, life and soul, Jerry's!

'Lynn, you are looking far too serious! Let's go back ten minutes to where we were before I spoke so very stupidly, and talk of other things!'

He gave her hand a gentle tap and put it back in her lap. It was as if he had given her back a part of herself and she was whole again . . . a strange thought, she told herself. Well, she would do as he suggested and resume their earlier conversation.

'You didn't answer my question, Philip. Will you go and see Marcia's baby for me?'

'It may not be very easy,' Philip said

awkwardly. 'By doing so I might make things very hard for Marcia. You and I . . . maybe even Jerry, might become involved . . .' He broke off but it was too late to take back the words. He saw incomprehension in Lynn's eyes and wondered how to tell her the truth as blurted out to him by the distraught girl.

'I'll tell you all I know if you give me your word of honour not to take any action without my agreement,' Philip said at last. 'I ought not to have told you so much, Lynn. I've already broken my promise to the girl.'

'I won't do anything without telling you,' Lynn said quickly.

'Well, it seems she met this man she is going to marry at the hotel in Devon where she was staying before the baby came. He only found out she was having a baby after he had fallen in love with her. When he got over the shock and learned she was unmarried, he offered to marry her after the baby was born on condition that she got rid of it. It sounds a bit brutal put that way but you can understand how he felt.

The fellow must have been pretty upset in the first place to find Marcia was having a child. It wouldn't be easy for a man to accept another man's child as his own unless . . . well, this man wouldn't.'

'But she always planned to have it adopted!'

'So she told me. She was intending to approach an agency or put herself in the hands of the Social Services before the child was born; but the new man in her life—a fellow she called Seymour—returned to London a fortnight before the baby was due; and when he didn't get in touch with her as he had promised, she panicked. She gave a false name at the hospital where she had the child; and discharged herself twenty-four hours later and took it up to London. By this time, her money was running out. She telephoned this Seymour chap from the station and discovered he'd been away on business and had not after all walked out on her. Understandably, he assumed she had left the baby in Devon. She was afraid to tell him she had the baby with her and leaving her suitcases at the station, she rushed off in an hysterical state of mind and left the infant in the first church she came to.'

Seeing the horrified expression on Lynn's face, he added gently:

'She swore to me she meant to go back for it and I believe her, Lynn. But this chap persuaded her not to do so; told her it would be well looked after and that by going back she would lay herself open to charges by the police and endless enquiries, and that his mother would make difficulties about their marriage if she discovered the truth. He persuaded her to remain at her flat, gave her money and has arranged things so they can be married almost immediately. Marcia met his mother and introduced him to her uncle and nothing can go wrong now, unless someone starts making enquiries and the police catch up with her. She's scared out of her wits, poor girl.'

Lynn digested this news with mingled horror, surprise and bewilderment.

'But I just don't understand,' she said at last. 'Jerry gave her money and she had a little of her own . . . an allowance from her uncle I think she said. She should have had enough to pay for the baby to be fostered.'

Philip bit his lip.

'She told me that your husband had promised the money, but that it never came!'

Lynn put her hands to her mouth.

'Oh, no! Jerry must have sent it. He must have done!'

'He probably sent it to the wrong address or something!' Philip said with a certainty he was far from feeling. 'In any case, you can see now why we mustn't do anything to jeopardize Marcia's position.'

'But the child, Philip. Don't you know that an abandoned child cannot be adopted? I read only recently in a magazine a long article about just that subject. The child is doomed now to life in an institution: I'm sure Marcia doesn't realize that. Besides, she will never have any peace of mind wondering if the police or authorities will one day trace her. She's young and she's been lonely and unhappy, Philip, so she acted in haste. I know she will regret it later. You must let me talk to her.'

Philip frowned.

'I hate to say this, Lynn, but you know I don't mean it against you, personally, but don't you think your family have disarranged her life enough as it is?'

Lynn clasped her hands in her lap, her face intent.

'That's just it, Philip. It's because "my family", as you term it, have been responsible for what has happened that I feel I must help her now. You said yourself she was disturbed, unhappy. If she felt she had done the right thing, surely she would be exactly the opposite? She's to be married soon so she ought to be on top of the world. She's a nice girl at heart. You must have seen that for yourself. I'm convinced she's feeling conscience-stricken and hunted. Let me go to her, Philip.'

'I've no right to come into this matter at all!' Philip said helplessly, wondering how he had allowed himself to become involved. 'I ought not to have told you so much.'

'Trust me, Philip! I'll talk to her as a friend. I'll guarantee her every protection if she will at least agree to giving her baby her name. There would be no need for her to tell the man she is to marry!'

'And supposing you do persuade her, what happens then?'

'Well, I presume the baby will remain in the care of an institution until a suitable couple come along to adopt it. Marcia may be

198

asked to contribute to its keep, but I'd do that willingly.'

'So I suppose you will want to see her as soon as possible.' It was more a statement than a question for he knew her well—knew that too much had been said for her to go home now, leaving the matter unresolved.

Lynn touched his hand impulsively, her eyes shining.

'I knew you'd understand, Philip. You always do!'

'Then here is what I suggest. I will telephone Marcia—she's living at her old flat. If she is willing to see you, the two of you can meet at my flat. You can't very well go to her place in case Seymour turns up to see her, and she can't go to your house. I shall make myself scarce and leave you to sort things out.'

Two hours later, she found herself face to face with Marcia in Philip's flat. They were quite alone and it was obvious to Lynn that the younger girl had been crying.

'I expected you'd want to see me!' were her first words to Lynn. 'I'm not sorry, really. I suppose that friend of yours told you after all?'

'I guessed most of it, Marcia,' Lynn said as she sat down opposite the younger girl. 'I didn't know that my husband had never sent you the money he promised. If it's true, I'm dreadfully ashamed.'

'I'm not,' the girl said with heightened colour. 'I'm glad he didn't or I should have taken it. But I hated the thought of accepting money . . . a kind of pay-off!' Her voice was bitter, desperately unhappy.

'Nevertheless, the lack of money must have made things harder for you. I thought about you so much, Marcia, when my own baby was coming, at his birth, afterwards. I couldn't stop wondering about you.'

'I thought about you, too!' the girl said, her voice suddenly soft. 'I saw in the *Telegraph* announcement that you'd had a boy. My baby was a little girl . . .' Suddenly her voice broke and she was sobbing brokenly. 'I've been so worried. The baby was beautiful. I would have loved her if I'd been able to keep her, but Seymour is adamant and I love him . . . I'm going to marry him. Oh, Mrs. Birch, do you think my baby will be all right? Night after night I wake up from terrible dreams about her. Suppose no one found her and she had starved to death . . . caught cold? Suppose she's being ill-treated, badly cared for? I know I ought not to have abandoned her but I was frightened . . . of losing Seymour . . . of everything.'

'My dear, what you did is understandable. You aren't the first person to do what you did! I blame myself. I asked you not to get in touch with Jerry ever again and you promised you would not do so . . . nor tell your family. Had you been able to ask for his help or had you had your family's advice, this might not have

200

happened. That's why I have come to help you.'

Gently, when Marcia was calmer, she outlined her plan for them to go together to the church where Marcia had left the baby. She, Lynn, would make enquiries as to where it had been taken, then see the person in authority and ask what would be the consequences if the baby's mother were to claim it as her own. Only if it was ascertained that no publicity or proceedings could affect Marcia's private life, need Marcia come forward.

Marcia dried her eyes. 'I brought her to London. The church was a little one called St. Stephens. We could go this afternoon . . .?'

Lynn breathed a sigh of relief.

'You're anxious to go, too now, aren't you, Marcia? I don't want to force you to do anything you don't really want to do.'

'No. I must go. I wanted to go before but I was afraid. I know I couldn't go through with my marriage to Seymour without knowing. He doesn't really understand why I worry so, and it would be such a bad start to our life together if there were any kind of uneasiness between us. He's been so marvellous to me in every way . . . standing by me. And I know he'd never reproach me. It's just that he can't understand why I am so worried. He thinks I did the best thing leaving her in a church.'

'He couldn't be expected to know that by

doing that your baby would always be denied a home life. You yourself were not aware of it so how should he, an ordinary nice young man, know such things?'

Philip was waiting outside the flat in his car. Briefly, Lynn told him what they planned to do and immediately he offered to drive them to the church. On the way there, he suggested to Lynn that he be allowed to ask his solicitor to act for Marcia should there be any chance of criminal proceedings.

'It shouldn't be necessary!' Lynn said. 'I remember that case in the paper about twins who were left on some doorstep and the mother was found later. I'm sure it said that it was not breaking a law to abandon your child.'

'But it's against the law of Nature!' Marcia whispered. 'I'm so afraid, Mrs. Birch . . . in case she should not be all right.'

They left Marcia in the car and together went to see the vicar of the little church. He remembered the baby immediately and told them that it had been taken to an associated children's home a mile away pending enquiries by the police. He asked no questions of them but did say:

'If anyone is in any trouble and I can be of help, please tell me.'

'Thank you!' Lynn said, realizing that he was probably thinking the baby was her child. 'We are not in any trouble and hope soon to put this matter right for the baby and its

202

mother.'

Half an hour later, she went alone to see the matron, and having gained an immediate promise from the kindly, grey-haired woman to treat what she said as a completely private confidence, she told her the whole story. She did not leave out Jerry's part in the telling for she knew it would lessen the blame for Marcia. She felt bitterly ashamed as she spoke but saw only pity, understanding, sympathy in the matron's quiet eyes.

'I see so many of these kinds of tragedies!' she said at last. 'It is always fear that makes women go against their own instinct, their own nature, in this way. It is the biggest contributory factor. Fear, and then ignorance. I don't think you need worry too much about this girl's future if she is willing to rectify her mistake. The baby is only . . . let me see . . . two months old? We shall find adopters without any difficulty. Your friend will have to prove the baby is hers, of course, so that it can be legally established it is her child. Then it is merely a matter of signing a form before a Justice of the Peace that she is willing to have the baby adopted. There would be no publicity of any kind. We would ask her meanwhile to contribute to the child's upkeep if she can while it is in our care.'

'I would like to do that!' Lynn said, and after a brief pause, added, 'Do you think it would be possible for me to see the baby?'

The matron gave her a quizzical glance and then stood up and put her finger on the bell. A young girl came in and was asked to fetch Baby Stephanie.

'That's our name for her!' she explained while they waited for the baby to be brought in. 'Because it was in the church of St. Stephen where she was found. She is a lovely-looking baby; they so often are. One wonders how mothers can bring themselves under any circumstances to part with them!'

The girl came back with a bundle in her arms which she gave at Matron's nod to Lynn. As she drew the shawl away from the baby's face, Lynn gave a little convulsive cry and the colour drained from her face.

'Oh!' she said on an indrawn breath. 'Oh, she's so very like my Paul!'

The likeness was indeed uncanny as neither child was like its father. Both babies had a fluff of fair hair and blue-grey eyes. Then Lynn recalled with sudden enlightenment that she and Marcia were alike. It was not really so extraordinary that Marcia's child and hers should resemble one another.

'It might be my baby's twin!' she said again when the young girl had gone and only the matron would hear her. 'There is a week between their birthdays and yet they are identical! I think I'd have believed this was Paul if I had found her in his cot at home.'

'They are alike only in looks!' Matron said

calmly. 'This baby has neither father nor mother nor brother nor sister. It is quite alone in the world!'

Afterwards, Lynn wondered if the older woman had said those words with the intention of rousing her maternal instincts. Or was it just Fate that had put the overwhelming thought in her mind . . . that she and Jerry must adopt this child?

While Marcia was having a somewhat tearful interview with the matron, Lynn sat in the car with Philip and told him what was in her mind. Philip looked deeply perplexed.

'I shouldn't be surprised that you should have had this notion!' he said immediately. 'I know you love kids, Lynn, and this baby is like Paul. But it cannot be undertaken lightly . . . even if your husband would consider it. Have you thought how he would react to such a suggestion?'

'No!' Lynn whispered, the fire of enthusiasm suddenly quenched, as Philip had assumed it would be. Then her lips set in a hard line of determination. 'He must be made to see that it's the *right* thing to do. The baby is his responsibility as much as Marcia's. And I want it, Philip! It seemed as I held her that she was in some way my baby . . . Paul's real twin. And she needs me; needs a father. We can give her everything that was denied her because of something Jerry should not have done. Can't you see this is what was meant to happen?'

'Oh, Lynn, my dear, you are so extraordinary I don't know what to say to you. Can *you* see that everything is mixed up? It ought to be the other way round . . . *your* husband asking you to take *his* child. It seems too fantastic . . . yet somehow typical of you that you should shoulder all the responsibility; all the consequences when you, really, are the one who was harmed most of all; who was the least to blame!'

'No, the baby was least to blame!' Lynn cried.

'Be that as it may, I can't bring myself to believe that Jerry is going to be enthusiastic about this idea, Lynn. I'd advise you to think very well about it before you go ahead with the idea of suggesting it. You must remember that you will be asking him to take into his home a living proof of his guilt. The baby might not seem that way to you, but I'm certain it will do so to him. It might come between you both. You might see it one day through his eyes and then you would have harmed the child far more than to let strangers have her.'

Lynn looked utterly downcast.

'I can't believe Jerry would feel that way . . . not if I really want the baby. I'd never reproach him or remind him of the fact that someone else was her real mother. I have no reproach in my heart now. He must realize it is his child . . his, Philip. Surely he could not deny paternity now?'

206

'It's your affair, Lynn, and I can't advise you. But do at least be prepared for him to greet your suggestion with anything but enthusiasm. Don't fly off the handle and tell him that it is his duty to do what you want in this matter. He may after all know what is best for you both.'

'Philip, if you were asked that same question, would you refuse to adopt this baby?'

'That is not a fair question, Lynn, but since you ask it, I personally could not refuse you anything you asked me. But I don't think your husband and I are very alike in temperament,' he added quickly to cover up the emotion in his voice and the implication she might draw from his words. 'Besides, the baby would bear no relationship to me, and as I have no children of my own, there would be no fear of my making any distinction between mine and this one.'

'But you think I would?'

Philip sighed.

'No, no, I don't think you capable of any such thing,' he said with a smile. 'But I'm biased in your favour, Lynn.'

'That's because you don't know me very well!' Lynn said with a quick smile. 'Dear Philip, if you lived with me for a week, you'd soon see that I was far from perfect!'

'I can think of nothing nicer than proving you right or wrong!' Philip said with a flippancy that eased the moment. He must really take a hold on himself, he thought.

Endearments, flattery, indications of the way he felt about her had been slipping out all too easily. He must take care not to offend her with his love. It could be such a nuisance when it was unwanted and he risked losing her, a fact which in itself was enough to make him guard his tongue and his heart more closely.

'I must ask Jerry, anyway,' Lynn said thoughtfully. 'I may be able to make him see things as I do . . . and he loves me, Philip. I'm quite sure of that. If I tell him how much this means to me, I think he will agree to let me adopt the baby. Somehow it seems as if I've known all along that this was what would happen. I once had a strange conversation about right and wrong with a woman I met in a park. She said that sooner or later one's bewilderment over a course of action always became clear . . . that one reached a moment where one knew positively that such a thing was right or wrong. I feel now with every fibre of my being that it would be right for me to take Marcia's baby as my child. Because of that feeling, I must tell Jerry . . . try to make him understand.'

'You must do what you think best, Lynn, and I'll hope for your sake that it all turns out as you wish it.'

Then Marcia came towards them, her face streaked with tears but strangely calm and peaceful.

'It's going to be all right!' she said. 'Matron
208

told me that this need not stand in the way of my wedding. I think she is hoping that perhaps in the end Seymour will agree to having my baby.'

'And you think that is possible?' Lynn could not refrain from asking. Yet she knew the answer even before Marcia said with utmost conviction:

'No! Nor would I ask him to. I want to forget . . . forget it ever happened. I want my marriage to Seymour to be a complete fresh start. I told Matron so and that it was for this reason I wouldn't see my baby. It's strange, I know, but already I feel that she isn't mine at all . . . that she's someone else's child.'

CHAPTER THIRTEEN

Lynn's natural impulse had been to rush home and tackle Jerry the instant he arrived back from work; but she curbed the wish because she could see there was something in Philip's warning to her. Jerry might not be at all happy about the idea of adding another child to the three they had. He had not been pleased when she had told him Paul was on the way. It would, undoubtedly, be quite a shock to him to hear that she had not only met Marcia but had been in touch with her since the baby's birth. A little voice inside her seemed also to be warning her that by nature Jerry would prefer not to have to accept a reminder of past misdeeds; that he would not stop to consider his moral responsibility for his child but only see it as a constant reminder of his own disgrace.

Gradually as she drew nearer to her home, her wish to speak to her husband of what had become so important to her now, became less and less a resolve, and she decided wisely to wait for the appropriate moment to bring up the subject. She would not blurt out everything in the first few moments but work up to it gradually, perhaps opening the subject by questioning him about the money he had promised to send Marcia. She felt a little shudder of distaste when it crossed her mind that, far from being lost in the post, that cheque might not even have been posted. But she rejected that thought. Jerry could not have been so mean.

She was greeted at her front door by Mary who told her that David and Sue were with their Aunty Marion, where she was about to call for them.

Lynn played for a moment with the idea of collecting them herself but she felt more than usually tired by the long and not uneventful day and so sealed a measure of her own fate by her decision.

She made herself a cup of tea and having refreshed herself, went upstairs to Paul's little room where he lay sleeping peacefully in his cot. She stood for a long time looking down at the tiny face and with a rush of tenderness at the minute little fist clenched against his smooth creamy cheek.

They are alike . . . amazingly so! she told herself. Both Jerry's children and yet both like me! It was a situation that might have been quite horrifying to another woman but to Lynn, who loved all children and whose maternal instinct far outweighed any other emotion in her, she could think of the baby— Marcia's baby—only with a deep longing. She imagined the second little cot here in this room beside her son's; imagined the two babies growing up side by side, laughing together, playing together and no doubt quarrelling, too! And to her they would be both equally lovable, equally dear.

She turned away and closed the door softly behind her. The momentary vision of the future had passed and left her tired again and strangely worried. It was because she had already guessed that Jerry's answer would be a definite "no" and that nothing she could say . . . no amount of pleading, would alter him.

Downstairs on the hall table she saw the afternoon post . . . two letters and a bill. She carried them into the sitting-room with another cup of tea and sat down to read them.

The first was a long letter from her aunt,

asking after the baby and the children, and stating her intention to visit them in a week or two's time.

I really must write to her! Lynn chided herself. I'll do it this evening!

Then she opened the other letter and started to read. But at the first words her heart began a frantic beating and the colour rushed into her cheeks.

'My darling,
Why haven't you answered my letters? What has happened to make you treat me like this? Oh, Jerry, if you only knew what agony of mind this silence on your part is causing me, you would not torture me so . . .'.

Lynn tore the letter away from her eyes and reached hurriedly for the envelope. Yes, it was addressed to Jerry and not to her! What a mad, crazy thing to have done . . . opening Jerry's letter without looking to see to whom it was addressed!

I won't read it! she said aloud, but her eyes would not obey her will and a moment later she was feverishly scanning the lines.

'I've asked myself a million times what can have happened. Has your wife found out? Have you met someone else? Are you ill? Away? When I ring your office, as I must have done at least six times, someone tells me you are "not in' and I've

*left three messages for you to ring my number.
Oh, darling, darling, I know I promised I would
never ring you there, I know it's dangerous, but
what else can I do? It's two whole weeks since
I heard a single word. Surely you would let me
know if something is wrong? Why don't you
telephone? I'm nearly mad with worry.*

*'Please, darling, don't be cross with me for
sending this to your home. I'm desperate . . .
almost too desperate to care if* she *finds out.
I suppose for your sake I hope she won't but I
must* know. *Darling, if it is all over between us,
then at least you could tell me so. You cannot
be such a coward as to leave things like this
after all we have meant to one another. Our last
meeting you told me you loved me. You can't
have stopped loving me so suddenly. What have
I done? What have I said? I know I ought to
have more pride than to write like this but where
you are concerned I have no pride left. You've
brought me down to the bottom of the pit, Jerry,
and what Heaven there has been between us is
now just one deep hell.*

*Write, ring, . . . but for pity's sake, Jerry, don't
leave me another day in this torture. I'll do
something crazy . . . crazier than sending this to
your home.*

Your ever-loving, mad, bad and very sad,

Betty'

I ought to faint or throw hysterics or burst
into tears! Lynn thought, but in fact she felt

emotionally stunned; completely and utterly numb. Only one thought was coherent . . . that this at long last was the end. She couldn't take any more. It was all over and finished. She could never, never forgive Jerry now. It had happened once too often and now the time had come for her to get out; leave him; divorce him; above all never see or speak to him again.

'Mummy, we're back! Sue and me's been playing Ludo. It's a smashing game. Can we buy a board for our own, Mummy?'

Her two children came into the circle of her arms and kissed her warmly on each cheek. Their own little faces were cold from the night air and flushed with excitement. They were very happy.

'Aren't you feeling very well, Mrs. Birch? You look ever so pale!'

'I'm rather tired!' Lynn said with an effort. 'It's been a tiring day.'

'Then you stay right where you are and I'll put the children to bed. Now come with Mary, lovies, and be good children because Mummy isn't feeling very well.'

'Might you be sick?' Sue asked curiously.

'No, Sweetheart! Now run upstairs with Mary, there's a good girl!'

David took her hand and held it for a moment in his own as if his child's intuition guessed something of her horror, her loneliness and her fear.

'You'll come and kiss us good-night,

Mummy?'

'Of course, darling!'

They had barely gone up the stairs with Mary before the front door banged and Jerry came in.

'Hullo, Sweet!' He came towards her but she quickly turned her face away from his kiss, her whole body tensed and icy cold. Silently, she held out the letter.

'What the—' He broke off as a dark red suffused his face and she saw that his hands were trembling as he held the thin pages in his fingers.

Talk yourself out of that one, Jerry! she thought with all the bitterness of disillusion! Let's see what you have to say to that!

'You had no right to read my private mail!'

'But I read it all the same, Jerry.'

He gave her a quick look of . . . was it curiosity? Had he expected something other than her cold, steady, toneless voice?

He turned away and went towards the drink cupboard.

That won't help you much! she thought as she watched him pour himself a double whisky and drink it neat.

'Well, what do you expect me to do, Lynn? Go down on my knees and beg you to forgive me?'

'No! I don't expect you to do anything or say anything. I'm going to divorce you, Jerry!'

His momentary truculence was replaced by

angry fear.

'You can't do that, Lynn. You can't do that!'

'Can't I, Jerry? I'm going to all the same.'

'You have no evidence . . .'

'But I have, Jerry. That letter is enough in itself.'

He glanced down at the letter he still held and then up at her. There was a tiny glow of triumph in his eyes.

'But that's not evidence of adultery. It's only an hysterical letter from an hysterical girl who happens to be in love with me.'

'You're denying you slept with her?'

'You couldn't prove it!'

'But I could, Jerry. I remember Betty very well! Judging from her state of mind I don't think I should have any difficulty in extracting a confession from her. And I also know where she lives. The only thing I don't know, Jerry, is when you found time to carry on this affair. You haven't been working late.' Her voice was full of scorn. 'You've been a model husband for months. I suppose you must have slipped out of your office for the occasional afternoon. Not that it matters now.'

'Lynn, you can't, you mustn't! It wouldn't be fair to that girl! It only happened once or twice. And what about the children? You've always said a broken home is the worst thing for kids.'

'It's better than their growing up to follow your example.'

216

'Lynn, I know I've behaved badly . . . disgracefully; that I gave you my word that this kind of thing would never happen again. But I couldn't help myself. I . . .'

'Jerry, please don't talk any more nonsense. Everyone is responsible for their actions. I've heard all this before. There is no excuse for what you've done . . . not once but over and over again. You disgust me!'

At last her voice broke and betrayed her feelings of despair. But curiously enough, she could think perfectly coherently, even to the extent that Jerry had not so far offered the sop that had so often succeeded in the past . . . those words, "I love you, Lynn, only you."

'Lynn, is there nothing I can do to make you change your mind? I know it is no use to say I am sorry . . . ashamed. But I don't want our marriage to break up. Is there nothing I can do or say to put things right?'

She looked at him for a long time, considering his words. Was there anything he could do? Anything at all? What kind of man was this to whom she had given her heart, her love, her life? What kind of weakling had she chosen as a father to her children?

'You know, I saw Marcia Henderson today . . . and her baby!' she said, more to herself than to him. He was obviously stunned by her words.

'Saw . . . who did you say?'

'Marcia Henderson . . . and your child. It's

very like Paul, only it's a little girl. I was going to ask you to let us adopt it.'

Jerry shrugged his shoulders in a masculine way which defied understanding of women.

'It beats me!' he said at last as he poured another whisky. 'You say you want to divorce me because of . . . well, a minor affair with another woman, yet you wanted to adopt my little bastard and throw it in with your own children.'

'Is it really so strange, Jerry? Can't you understand that I could forgive a mistake once . . . accept it a second and, yes, a third time, but there has to be a limit to the number of times any woman will allow her husband to make love to other women!'

He jumped at the first loop-hole she had offered him. 'Then you still love me?'

'I have loved you very much . . . enough to want to take on your child as my own, Jerry, if that is proof enough. But as to whether I love you now . . . I think I hate you. I hate you for the humiliation of *that*!' She pointed to the letter, her face white now with emotion that had begun to threaten her calmness and destroy the numbness of the first shock.

'And you believe I haven't loved you just as much as you loved me?'

'No, I don't think you know the meaning of the word!' Lynn cried. 'You've wanted me, Jerry, passionately! And you needed a wife to minister to your comfort and provide a home and family background for you. But I don't think you can have come near to loving me or you could not have hurt me and risked losing me and your children by these horrid, sordid little affairs. I think it might have been easier for me to bear if you had at least cared a little for these . . . these women. But they meant nothing at all to you . . . or so you always tell me. And for that, you spoil our love, our marriage . . . maybe even our children's lives.'

He walked away from her and absent-mindedly drew the curtains that so far no one had thought to draw against the darkening sky.

'I don't think you've ever realized quite how difficult marriage is for me!' he said at last. 'I'm not naturally a faithful person, I suppose. I've tried to behave reasonably and I know I've failed badly but I've done my best. You say I could have helped myself . . . that I should have had more control over my actions. But I've tried, Lynn. I wanted to be a good husband and father and be worthy of you. But you're too damned good for me, I suppose. No one *could* live up to *your* standards!'

'That's not true!' Lynn cried involuntarily. 'I haven't asked much of you, Jerry . . . only that you should keep the vows you made on our wedding day. How could you? I just don't understand how you could do it if you loved me. Is it just weakness? Must you always have what you want irrespective of the cost to me . . . to other people? I'm as sorry for those girls

219

as I am for myself. Betty Smart. Too desperate to care whether or not I did read that letter. What do you do to them that they love you so much? And Marcia Henderson . . . look at the untold misery you've caused her. And since we're talking of her . . . please don't lie to me, Jerry . . . did you or did you not send her that cheque?'

'If you've talked to her you probably know that I didn't send it. But damn it all, Lynn, why should I? I couldn't even be sure that it was my child; that I was responsible.'

'That's a mean, dirty thing to say, Jerry. She loved you, too. And if ever you saw her child, you'd know it must be yours. The likeness to Paul is extraordinary.'

'And you want us to adopt it?'

'I did want that, Jerry! If you'd agreed to let me have her, I'd have been so happy. But not now. Now our life together is finished and I want nothing but a divorce.'

His voice became pleading.

'Lynn, don't say that. You can't mean it . . . not after all these years. You know I never dreamed it would come to this. Is there nothing I can do or say that will make you change your mind? Haven't you a spark of feeling left for me?'

'I don't see why you shouldn't welcome a divorce yourself, Jerry. Then you'd have the freedom to behave exactly as you please. For what reasons do *you* want our marriage to continue? I can't find any.'

'You know how fond I am of David, Sue . . . '

'Yes. But that's hardly enough, is it, Jerry?'

'You know how I love you, Lynn!'

'I don't know it. I can't believe in your love any more, Jerry. And I don't want that kind of love . . . if love it really is. I'd rather be without you. I'd rather admit defeat.'

'Perhaps *you* want *your* freedom? What about this man Philip, whom you seem so attached to? You've had your fun so why should you deny me the right to the same?'

She felt wildly angry with him and her voice rose as she said:

'I have not been having that kind of "fun", Jerry! Philip is a good friend and there has only been friendship between us.'

'You deny then that the fellow is in love with you?'

She bit her lip.

'No, I believe he is. But he has known all along that I regarded him only as a friend; wanted him only as a friend. That's all there has been to it.'

'It's a pity I didn't know that sooner!' Jerry said easily. 'You see, Lynn, I had begun to believe you were in love with him. I was jealous and I thought it a bit steep after all you said to me about my having a girl friend that you should turn round and produce a boy friend at the time when I was trying to build up our life together. More fool me, I suppose, I should have known better.'

'You should have known me better!' Lynn said. 'Oh, Jerry, don't let's go on talking like this I can't stand any more. Even if you thought I was in love with or falling in love with Philip, that is no excuse for . . . for Betty Smart.'

'I wasn't offering it as an excuse. I was merely trying to explain how it happened after the promises I made you. But you don't wish to see that. You want to get rid of me and I suppose I don't blame you.'

'Jerry! That's a lie. I've never wanted to be rid of you. I've loved you with all my heart; believed in you, forgiven you, trusted you. Why should I want my marriage to end like this? What have I got to gain? Don't you think I'll be lonely? And don't you think my task of looking after the children by myself will be difficult? Don't you realize that I'll be hard-up, living on the alimony you'll have to pay me? Don't you think I am horrified at the thought of all a divorce means?'

'Then for pity's sake, Lynn, give it another trial. Don't act in haste. I hadn't meant to tell you this but I've a new job lined up. A divorce at this juncture might ruin everything. Even if you can't bring yourself to make a fresh start, then at least for my sake . . . and yours, too, in the end, let us carry on as before until this job is landed. It's worth a great deal to me. If after a month or so you still wish to go ahead with the divorce, then I suppose I have no right to stand in your way. It'll make your position easier and it will benefit the children.'

'I suppose that is reasonable,' Lynn said weakly. 'All right, Jerry, we'll wait a couple of months. Maybe in that time I shall have been able to think more clearly. *But I cannot believe I shall ever want to be a wife to you again.*'

And as if it were her theatrical cue to come in on those words, Mary opened the door and announced calmly:

'Dinner is ready, Mrs. Birch I rang the bell but you didn't hear and the soup is getting cold.'

Almost silently and without mirth, Lynn began to laugh.

CHAPTER FOURTEEN

'Lynn, if you do divorce him, will you marry me?'

Lynn looked at the man waiting so anxiously for her reply and tears of weakness and worry came into her eyes. It was three days since she had had the ultimate blow, three days of too much thinking, feeling; three nights of too little sleep. She felt utterly tired, spent, exhausted.

'Philip, you know I couldn't. I hate to say it like this but . . . well, I don't love you.'

'You're still in love with him?'

'I don't know. Perhaps it's just that I've loved him so long it's a habit. I just don't know.'

'If only you'd let me take care of you and the children! I'd ask nothing more than that. We'd live in the Manor House. You thought it so beautiful there, Lynn. And the children liked it and they like me. And I'd be only too willing to adopt Marcia's baby if you still want her.'

'Philip, don't tempt me. I'm so tired. You offer me peace and security and a way out. But it wouldn't be right . . . you know that. There must be love on both sides.'

'And you could never learn to love me?'

'I don't know, Philip. I don't think I ever want to fall in love again. It's too terrible a thing when it goes wrong. I've loved Jerry so much, Philip. How could he do this to me? How could he?'

He didn't try to answer a question to which he himself did not know the answer. He could have said that he believed Jerry Birch to be utterly unworthy of her love; that he knew the man to be weak and amoral. But deep down, the conviction that it was wrong to say anything that might influence a wife against her husband still held him mute. It warred with his own passionate desire for her; his own love for her. He, too, felt spent by the battle of his emotions.

224

'I still can't believe it's over . . . finished with!' she said thoughtfully. 'Oh, Philip, it's such a mess!'

He looked at her face with compassion and understanding.

'It needn't be over if you don't wish it so, Lynn. You can forgive him . . . have another try. You still love him, don't you? In spite of everything!'

'No! I couldn't forgive him again. I couldn't go on like this year after year forgiving and making fresh starts and knowing all along that the same thing would happen again sooner or later. It's just because I've been so happy, Philip! He's been a wonderful husband between times. We were both happy . . . very happy. I'd have given him anything in the world he wanted. But I'm not willing to share him.'

She turned her head and remembered suddenly the man to whom she was talking. She laid her hand on his arm and said gently:

'Forgive me, Philip. You are the last person in the world to whom I should be speaking like this. Do you know that Jerry was actually jealous of you?'

'I wish there had been some cause for his jealousy!' Philip said with a wry grin. 'Whatever else you worry about, Lynn, don't please add me to the list. You know I am fully aware of how you feel about me and I'm more than content to be nothing more than a friend . . . if that is all you need from me. I would not have asked you to marry me except that I did want you to know that you would always have a home waiting. And I wanted to tell you the children would be just as greatly loved as yourself. I wouldn't be "putting up" with them for the sake of winning you. I'm really very attached to them. David reminds me sometimes of my youngest brother, Martin, and Sue . . . well, who could help loving Sue?'

'You're a dear, Philip! I wish so much that I had been able to fall in love with you. How happy I could have been!'

Silence fell between them and leaning over the steering wheel of his car where they had parked miles from anywhere in the Chilterns, he stared out of the misty window into the cold, bleak twilight.

'It's time to take you home!' he said at last. 'We can't stay here all night, Lynn, much as I should enjoy it.'

'Oh, Philip, I can't go home and face the children. David, particularly, is so intuitive. He guessed there was something upsetting me although he couldn't begin to know what. When Jerry left the house after breakfast and I went downstairs, he was getting ready for school. He slipped his hand in mine and said, "I love you, Mummy!" Just like that . . . for no reason. I felt like bursting into tears.'

'Perhaps they will be in bed by now!' Philip suggested. 'It's half past six.'

'Then I suppose they will. Mary has been so marvellous. I think she does know something is wrong although she never asks questions. I've wanted for some time to have Mary live with us. At present she lives with an elderly relation. She has no one else in the world and I think she'd like to come. Maybe she will if she can find someone to look after the old aunt.'

She broke off suddenly and, to Philip's consternation, tears began to roll down her cheeks. She cried quietly for a moment or two, then, with an effort, wiped her tears away and said in a choked little voice:

'I find it so hard to realize that everything will be different now. I may not be able to afford Mary; and I shall have to find another house. Philip, I honestly don't think I've got the courage to go. What will I say to the children? How can I explain?'

'Perhaps you should not go at all, Lynn,' Philip said. 'I don't think in your heart you really wish it that way. I believe that if you really wanted this to be the end, you'd have gone by now . . . walked out of the house with the children and blown the consequences. Isn't that true?'

She did not answer him for a moment. Then she said:

'I suppose that is true. When I read Betty's letter I felt that way . . . as if everything was finished. I knew I wanted to divorce Jerry and that's all I thought about.'

'Then you talked it over with him?'

'Yes. I suppose I began to weaken. I don't know. I agreed to stay for a couple of months at least until he got this job. I didn't even ask what it was because I didn't really care. Maybe I didn't mind about it . . . just wanted an excuse to put off any immediate action that would be irrevocable. I'm so weak, Philip, where Jerry is concerned. I began to ask myself, have I failed him? Is it my fault? Would he have been different if he'd been married to someone else? Could I have prevented it? One can always find a loophole. This time I realized that I had been partially responsible. You see, I engaged Betty Smart, knowing she was attractive and that I should be leaving them alone in the house together. But you see, I trusted him. Perhaps that wasn't fair of me . . . knowing how these things happen to Jerry. The feminine sex don't seem able to leave him alone and he's weak. I ought to be strong for him and help him guard against that weakness.'

The man listening to her did not make any reply. He could not do so without telling her his real opinion of Jerry Birch. And it was more than clear to him that Lynn still loved him; or at least believed herself to be still in love with him even while her lips denied it.

'You said just now you didn't think you had the courage to go, Lynn. Have you the courage to make another start?'

228

'I don't know!' Lynn whispered. 'But I think I'll try, Philip. I think for the children's sake . . . and for mine, too, I'll try.'

'Where there's a will there's a way!' Philip said quietly. 'I'll take you home now . . . and Lynn, promise me you'll come to me if you get desperate . . . the way you did today? I'd be so worried if I thought you'd forbear to confide in me because . . . well, because you know how I feel about you. Promise?'

'I promise, Philip . . . and thank you!'

It was his one measure of consolation for the loss of something he had dared hope for one brief moment to win.

*   *   *

She lay awake in the darkness listening to the slow breathing of the man at her side. Gently, so that she should not wake him, she reached out and touched his side. The tenderness that was in her was so enveloping that she felt he must wake and be aware of it. But he slept on like a child.

'Can it be only four weeks ago that I was going to divorce him?' she asked herself in utter incredulity. This was the man she loved . . . her first love and her enduring love. There could never be anyone else. And in spite of everything, she did still love him with an absorbing, passionate, and maternal tenderness that had withstood all the injuries he had inflicted on her.

She marvelled a little at the power of love. Then her thoughts swung back to the events that had brought her here, to this hotel room, into this luxurious bed with Jerry by her side.

It had been his wish that they come here . . . his last effort to break down her resistance . . . and he had won. The victory had all been his. He had staked everything on this last chance and she was glad, glad, glad that the gamble had won out in his favour.

'You say you can't feel anything for me any more, Lynn; that you're emotionally dead; that I've killed all feeling in you. Let me prove it isn't true, darling. Let me show you that it can be as perfect as it has ever been between us . . . in every possible way. Give me this last chance to prove how much I still love you, need you, long for you.'

'It wouldn't be any use, Jerry. I just can't feel anything any more. I'm not willing to go on as we are. I don't care for this state of affairs any more than you do.'

The awkward conversations in front of the children, the keeping up a pretence of everything being normal in front of Mary, Marion, their other friends; the long, desperate, uncomfortable silences between them when they were alone were a shocking strain on her nervous system. It hadn't been entirely true that she had felt emotionally numb. She had meant only that she had felt immune to Jerry physically. In fact she had felt an endless tugging at her mind to settle things one way or another. One day she would feel that she must go . . . get away from Jerry once and for all and try to begin again by herself; the next day she would seriously consider trying to begin again with Jerry.

'I can't bear it any more!' Jerry had said at last. 'I've got to have you back, Lynn. You can't expect me to go on living here in the house beside you and behave as if we were complete strangers. It must be all or nothing between us; you must see that. We've been too near to each other in the past to put up with a half-and-half arrangement like this. At least give me a chance, Lynn. Come away with me for a week-end. I give you my word I won't force you to anything you don't wish. If when the time comes you feel you cannot face it, then I shall have to realize that I've lost you. But I can't . . . won't think of anything so awful. Come away with me, Lynn. Give me forty-eight hours alone with you, away from this house and all its memories. Give me the chance to prove that love is still there.'

Love . . . or passion? Was it either or both which had won the day for Jerry? He had wooed her all over again just as he had done when they'd first met. She had discovered that even while her mind resisted him and his charm and charming ways, her body had answered him with dreadful purpose, unquestionable acceptance.

And now she was glad! Jerry would not have gone to such immense thought and trouble to bring them together again if he had not loved her. She could believe now that he did so in spite of his acts of unfaithfulness. She could believe now that he had committed those acts against his better instincts, and that it was up to her in future to protect him from women like Betty Smart.

He stirred at her side and then yawned sleepily and opened his eyes. She looked at him a little shyly and held out her hand.

'Must be getting late. I ordered breakfast in bed . . . thought you might like a lie-in for a change. You never have the chance at home.'

'That was sweet of you, darling. It's going to be a lovely day . . . sunny and bright. I love it when it's frosty and cold and the sun is shining. Let's go for a walk later, Jerry!'

'We'll see!' he said, reaching for and lighting a cigarette.

There was a knock on the door and the maid came in with a breakfast tray. Jerry spoke to her about the weather and the surrounding countryside and asked her advice about the best places to enjoy a nice long walk.

When the girl left Lynn started to sort out the plates and pour the coffee. Jerry, however, got out of bed and started to dress.

'You're going to have yours when you're dressed?' Lynn asked, watching him take off his pyjama jacket and run the water into the basin and begin to shave.

'Uh-huh!'

She spread the butter on her toast and asked:

'Where shall we walk, Jerry? Inland, or by the sea?'

'Neither!'

She looked up from the breakfast tray in surprise at the vehemence in his voice.

'Don't you feel up to it, darling?'

'We're going home, Lynn.'

'But, Jerry, why? You said you'd booked for two nights. I don't understand . . .'

'Don't you? Well, my dear, the brief little holiday has served its purpose. I brought you here because I wanted to be quite certain that you could not go through with your plan to divorce me. You see, I have too much at stake to risk that.'

'I still don't understand!' she whispered, aghast at the tone of his voice.

'No? Well, it probably did not occur to you that last night you negated any previous act of unfaithfulness by me. If you tried to divorce me now, Lynn, I'd contest it whatever the grounds you gave. You probably noticed that I chatted a long time with the maid. Didn't you wonder why? I merely wanted to make quite sure she would remember us . . . the loving couple in the double bed. So you see, there's no further reason for staying here. As soon as

233

you're up, I suggest we pack our suitcases and go home.'

So, in a matter of minutes, he killed once and for all the deep well of her love for him. She looked at him, seeing him now as he really was, and knew that here finally was something she would never forgive. She would never love him again.

* * *

'You'll get over it in time, Lynn dear! Try to believe that. In a little while none of this will seem so terrible!'

So Marion had tried to console her the day she had returned from that farcical week-end with Jerry; the day when she had started her preparations to leave him for always.

She could smile, if a little wryly, these few months later, to recall how infuriated she had been that she could not stride dramatically out of the house slamming the front door behind her as did the 'wronged' women in films, plays, books. When it came to reality, she discovered that it took time to leave your old life and a good deal of planning to begin a new one!

Perhaps during those early days when she had been too busy to think very much about anything but the practical all-too-necessary domestic details, she had believed Marion's assurance that she would mind less in the future. In any case, she was riding on a crest of hurt dignity, anger, injured pride and an intense desire to revenge herself on Jerry. Divorce him she could not, but leave him she could and would.

In that frame of mind, she had followed him into the house, going straight to her room to telephone Marion, asking if she could possibly put up the two older children for a night or two. Marion, as always the perfect friend, asked no questions and simply told Lynn to send Mary round with David and Sue as soon as she wished.

Ignoring Jerry who was pouring himself a drink in the sitting-room, Lynn went past him to the nursery to be greeted with shouts and hugs from the children who had not expected them back until the next day.

A little of her new-found determination and self-assurance left her as they rushed past her to find Jerry. Was it, after all, fair to part them from their father? Had she the right? Then her lips twisted with the memory of Jerry's behaviour and she lifted her head and started to explain to Mary that she and Mr. Birch had decided to live apart for a while and until she found a flat, Mary was to go to Mrs. Castle with David and Sue.

Mary had taken this somewhat unexpected piece of news with her usual calm. (Maybe she had been expecting it, Lynn thought bitterly. Living so close to them, perhaps Mary had seen further than she herself had done.)

'Perhaps it would be best for me to take Paul, too, seeing as how you'll want to be free to go house hunting?'

'Well, if you're sure you can manage . . .'

When the children ran back into the playroom, Lynn told them quietly that they would be spending the night with Aunty Marion.

'Aren't you and Daddy coming, too?' David asked, sensing something odd in her manner with that curious intuition he seemed always to have for her moods.

'I'll be coming, darling, but not Daddy. Now don't ask questions, please, David. Just do as Mary tells you and go and pack up the toys you want to take with you!'

'Are we going to stay a *long* time?' asked Sue, for they did not usually take their toys to Marion's for short visits as she had a box of games she kept especially for their afternoons there.

'Now come along, Ducks, and leave Mummy alone. She's very tired and she has lots to do!' Mary answered for Lynn.

They'll have to be told sooner or later! Lynn thought wretchedly as she went to her own bedroom to start packing. Then she put that problem away from her for the more immediate one of where they would live and how she was going to manage financially. With every part of her being, she shrank from having to ask Jerry for money! Had it not been

236

for the children, she could have walked out of the house and if necessary found a job to support herself. She would rather a hundred times over do that than accept so much as a farthing from him.

But even at that moment, she could think unemotionally; could see that she could not possibly hope, unskilled as she was, to support three children and Mary and herself. For their sake, she must forgo the luxury of pride and take every penny she could get from Jerry.

They had not spoken since that bitter scene in the hotel. Once or twice Jerry had tried to say something but she had sealed her lips tightly, knowing that if she said anything at all, she would lose her self-control and say far too much.

Once, on the drive home, Jerry had said:

'Look here, Lynn, I'm sorry to have had to do that. You won't hold it against me, will you? I suppose it was a mean trick but honestly, I had to do it. You wouldn't promise me *not* to get a divorce and my whole future career depends to a large extent on your decision. I can't explain in detail but you'll see for yourself later on, if what I hope will happen comes off. I'm not asking you to forgive me or anything like that. I know you must hate me now but believe me, I'm really doing this for your sake and the children's . . .'

It was the last straw, and knowing that if he continued she would scream or do something equally hysterical, Lynn broke in saying furiously:

'If you don't stop talking, I shall get out of the car and go home by train!'

He must have heard by the tone in her voice that she was near breaking point. At any rate, he said no more.

Now, suddenly, he came into her bedroom, and seeing the suitcases and clothes strewn on the bed, said sharply:

'What are you doing, Lynn?'

'Leaving!'

'But what's the point in doing that?'

'There's such a thing as separation. I'm leaving you, Jerry.'

He lit a cigarette and sat down on the bed.

'Now don't be silly, Lynn! Why on earth walk out like this?' By his tone of voice, he might have been discussing the merits of a play or a summer holiday.

'Because I don't wish to have to see you, Jerry, nor speak to you for as long as I live.'

He gave a short laugh.

'Okay! If that's how you feel. But why the hurry? We've been through situations like this before now and lived quite comfortably under the same roof without speaking to each other.'

Can he imagine that I'll get over it this time just as I did those other times? She swung round to face him, her arms clasping a neat pile of folded underwear—flimsy, glamorous wisps of nylon and lace which she had chosen because Jerry liked them! But she was unaware of what she held.

'There has never been a situation like this before, Jerry. Those other times I was hoping for a reconciliation. This time I am not. Perhaps you weren't aware of the fact that last night I had no intention of divorcing you? That I'd quite forgiven you for the umpteenth time? So what you did was unnecessary as well as despicable.'

She turned quickly away from him, fearing he might see the tell-tale tears that had sprung to her eyes.

'I can quite understand why you should be feeling the way you do!' Jerry said smoothly. She was astounded at the casualness of his tone of voice. 'All the same, rushing out of the house like this is really rather—'

He broke off as a knock came at the door.

Lynn walked across and opened it.

'We're just off, Mrs. Birch. I've packed most of the things the children will need for tonight and tomorrow and I can always run round and get anything else they need.'

'Very well, Mary, I'll see you later!'

For the first time, Jerry looked and sounded ill-at-ease. Was this the first time he believed she intended to leave him; really understood that this time she was going?

'Where are you taking the children, Lynn? I insist on knowing.'

'They are going to Marion's with me!' Lynn

said quietly.

'You've no right—' Jerry began, when she broke in:

'I'm not concerned with "rights", Jerry, although I suspect that I have more of them than you under the circumstances.'

'I forbid you to take the children out of his house!'

Downstairs a door banged and Lynn almost smiled at Mary's timing. It might have been the end of a scene in a play.

'They've gone, Jerry. And since I have no intention of standing here discussing the matter with you, I'll tell you this . . . that if you try to interfere in any way in my life from now on, or the children's lives, I shall take this whole affair to court and obtain a judicial separation. Seeing that you are so very anxious to avoid publicity, presumably you won't want that. Now will you please go?'

Jerry's face was suffused with an angry red. He jumped up and strode across the room, grabbing Lynn's arm in a grip that hurt. She bit her lip and stood calmly while he raved.

'They are my children as much as yours. I have the right to say what they shall do . . .'

She let him finish and then, dragging her arm free, said:

'I'll let you know through our lawyer, Jerry, when it is convenient for you to see David and Sue and Paul. Frankly I don't think you really care very much if you see them or not.

240

You just hope to get at me by insisting on your "rights". Well, I shan't stop you seeing them because I don't think anything that has happened between us should be allowed to hurt them. I shall say nothing against you and if you, Jerry, ever try to influence them against me in any way, however small, I shall make it my business to prevent you seeing them at all. Now get out, *get out!*'

Well, he hadn't tried to see them after all. In the days that followed, he had left the large empty house and taken a service flat in London. Their lawyer had written giving her his change of address. He had also instructed her that Jerry gave her full authority to sell the house if she didn't wish to live in it and had made the deeds over in her name.

But she could not go back. She had already found a large unfurnished maisonette on the ground floor of a converted house, with full use of the gardens for the children. When she heard from the lawyer, she signed the contract for a leasehold for one year with the option of renewing. She had been worried about furnishing the flat but now that she could sell the house, she could take from it what furniture they needed.

Jerry had also been generous about money. He had opened a separate bank account for her at their bank and advised her that she could draw on it as she wished up to a given amount a month.

'He's trying to make amends!' Marion and Jack had said.

'Or trying to ease his conscience!' Lynn replied bitterly.

But whatever he did now or in the future, she knew she could never love him again. She might only hate him a little less.

Once they had moved into the flat, which was no mean task and took all her time and energy, leaving none for brooding, reaction set in. Staring round the strange walls, seeing the different view from the windows, hearing the different sounds that are peculiar to every dwelling place, she knew that while she had succeeded in making some kind of home for the children, she had only succeeded in putting a roof over her own head. This could never be home to her.

Mercifully the children had been so excited by the move and exploring their new rooms and the new garden, they had scarcely missed Jerry. She had told them briefly that Daddy had to live in London for a little while to be near his work as he was very busy, and they had accepted it as children will.

But she missed him! She could not cast off the habit of seven years in seven weeks. She had to fight against the thought that Jerry would be home at seven and she must prepare dinner for him; had to remind herself that there were, after all, no shirts to be washed and ironed; no need to order his favourite rump steak from the butcher!

At night she lay awake hour upon hour, too tired to read but too restless to sleep. She did not want him back; never once did she wish to put back the clock, and yet she could see no happiness in the future, only a terrible loneliness. Philip, good friend that he was, had been a tower of strength, taking the children off her hands during the move, at the auction; advising her about laying lino and carpets, storing excess furniture, explaining legal documents. He had in his own way done all that he could to make her life brighter. There were flowers everywhere the day they moved in. There were presents for the new playroom and a wonderful hamper of food from Harrods so that they need not cook for at least two days!

But since they had moved in, she had found herself refusing his invitations to dinner just as she refused Marion's and Jack's many requests for her to join them of an evening. It was as if she were afraid of their pity although they offered none; as if she knew that she must fight this bad spell alone.

If it had not been for the placid, friendly sympathy of Mary who was now living in, Lynn felt she might have had a complete breakdown.

It was Mary, carrying on just as she had always done as if nothing at all out of the ordinary had occurred, that steadied her own nerves and forced her to behave and act as if she, too, were living an ordinary life instead of walking round knowing that her life was broken into a hundred irreplaceable pieces.

It was January when finally Jerry came to see her. For the children's sake, Lynn had made every effort to see their Christmas was in no way lessened by Jerry's absence. She had Marion and Jack and Philip to spend the day with them, and Philip, as ever, was just the right person to dress up as Father Christmas; to dispense the tree presents; to carve the turkey; to order and buy the wine. And because the children so obviously did not miss Jerry owing to Philip's replacement of their father, and had loved every second of their day, she had been happy, too; or at least, outwardly so. Inside she knew herself to be dead to any emotion. She was unable to feel.

Then one cold, dark evening when she was sitting alone in the sitting-room sewing, Mary came in and told her that Jerry had called and asked to see her.

'I could say you are out if you want, Mrs. Birch!'

Lynn shook her head. Had she feared that she might weaken in her resolve to be finished with Jerry for good, she might have feared to meet him. But she was not afraid.

In her darkest, most despairing moments, she had never for one instant believed she could love him again.

'Show him in, Mary!'

She watched him with curious eyes as he came into the unfamiliar room, looking around him with interest.

'I must admit you were always rather hot on *decor*,' he said smiling at her. 'I thought the outside looked rather gloomy and depressing but I must say this is very attractive!'

'Won't you sit down, Jerry?'

He looked a little taken aback by her coolness of tone but he sat down and lit a cigarette. Part of her mind recalled that this was the silver cigarette case she had given him on their first wedding anniversary. Inside it was inscribed: *'To Jerry, With all my love, Lynn'!*

'I came to see you because I'm going abroad, Lynn. I thought we ought to discuss one or two matters.'

He was watching her face but she continued with her sewing and appeared unmoved by his announcement.

'Yes?'

'As a matter of fact, I'm going to America. I've got a new job there. If it works out as I hope, I'll probably stay over there. In fact I might even take out naturalization papers for American citizenship!'

A little of her surprise broke through the mask on her face. He saw it and laughed.

'You know me, Lynn. I'm on to a good thing and it may pay me to become an American. As a matter of fact, I anticipate being in the money from now on so you and the

245

children should get about twice your present allowance.'

'That's very generous of you, Jerry.'

'Aren't you going to congratulate me?' He smiled at her with all his old charm. She saw it but was untouched by it. 'Should I congratulate you?'

'Now don't get shirty, my dear! You know very well you don't care what I do or where I go, so why be nasty when what I happen to be doing, benefits you, too?'

'I'm not very interested in your future, Jerry. If that's all you came to discuss, I suggest you go!'

'Well, as a matter of fact, it involves you. You see, I want a divorce!'

Lynn could not conceal her surprise. *When he had gone to such lengths to prevent her divorcing him!*

'Well, you see, this new job is tied up with a woman. I suppose you guessed as much.'

'As a matter of fact, I didn't!' Lynn said. But she knew now that she ought to have done.

'An American girl called Lola Vandink. Her father is the owner of the Vandink canning business and a multi-millionaire. He's promised me a starting salary of £60,000 a year, in dollars, on the understanding I marry Lola as soon as I'm free. It seems too lucrative a job to chuck away, doesn't it? I'm hoping Lola will become less possessive once the novelty of an English husband wears off. At

246

the moment, of course, she's rather unbearably in love with me. Still, no doubt she'll cool off once she's got me tied and then I hope I'll have a bit of freedom. In time I hope to make myself so indispensable to old Vandink that I shall get substantial rises in position and salary and eventually, of course, the millions that will be Lola's.'

He broke off to throw his cigarette into the fire.

'I suppose this all sounds rather mercenary to you, Lynn. You were always such a hopeless romantic. But you know, plenty of money can make even the most difficult of marriages work. And it'll compensate me for leaving dear old England . . . and, of course, the kids.'

Is that all David and Sue and Paul mean to him? Lynn asked herself.

Something of her thoughts must have shown in her face for he said:

'I hate leaving them. It may be years . . . oh, well, no doubt it's for the best. I suppose I'm not much of an example to them. In fact I can quite see that I'm not cut out either for a husband or a father! I hate too many ties. Love ought to be a free thing. It was free until society tied it down with chains. You know, I loved you more than any other woman I've ever known, Lynn. I'm sorry it didn't work out. I suppose we were never very well suited. I found your high moral standards impossible to live up to, and you aren't exactly the type to work a "live-and-let-live" arrangement.'

'If you mean that I should have stood by while you had one woman after another in your bed, no!'

He stood up, smiling faintly. It seemed to Lynn that his smile had become fixed on his face. Maybe it wasn't quite so easy to say goodbye as he wished to pretend. This *was* goodbye, wasn't it?

'You won't contest a divorce, Lynn? After all, *you* may want to marry again yourself. And cash in the bank meanwhile will help see the children through school and that kind of thing.'

'I wouldn't refuse a divorce in any case, Jerry. I'll be glad to be free of you!'

'I can understand your being bitter!' Jerry said, but she knew that he'd had hopes of a sentimental farewell. She held out her hand.

'Well, thanks for everything, Lynn. Sorry I made such a mess of things. Remember me sometimes.'

'Good-bye, Jerry!'

He stood for a moment looking down at her with a puzzled expression on his face as if he did not understand her any more. He must have known in that moment that any power he had once had to move her was quite gone.

Then she drew her hand away and went past him to open the door. He walked through it and when he turned round, the door had closed again, shutting her away from him.

He shrugged his shoulders and ignoring Mary's look as she handed him his coat, he went out into the darkness and felt the wind howl round the corner of the street. He had got Lynn's promise to divorce him, which was the reason for his coming, but the victory had turned sour in his grasp.

*   *   *

'Lynn, will you marry me?'

She felt sick with unhappiness . . . with hopelessness as she replied to him without hesitation:

'Philip, my dear, I can't! I've thought about it believe me, I *have* thought about it a very great deal. I would like to marry you . . . but I just can't.'

'Why not, Lynn?'

'Because I don't love you, Philip. I like you, I admire you, I respect you, I trust you absolutely; I think you would make a wonderful father for my children, but . . .'

'But you don't love me as you loved Jerry?'

She nodded her head dumbly.

'Yet what you just said you felt for me included all those ingredients I believe make up the most perfect form of love!'

'But, Pip, love is something else . . . something more. It's that strange feeling one has for another human being . . . a feeling of belonging; a kind of instinct; a kind of bond that draws two people together.'

'But that could be no more than physical attraction! And you spoke of instinct, Lynn. Did your instinct make you judge what was best for you? Knowing what you know now about Jerry, can you say you ever "belonged" as kindred spirits?'

She stared at him wide-eyed.

'But Pip, when I fell in love, I believed we were just that!'

'Exactly! You loved only what you believed him to be, wanted him to be. I would not want to be loved by you as you loved Jerry! No, I would not want a blind, unseeing devotion. You see me, know me, as I am; yet you still like me, respect me, trust me. Do you think that kind of love is less than you offered your husband? Can't you see that it would be far, far more?'

'But Pip if that is true and I do marry you, I should still have the feeling deep down inside me that you cared more about me than I do about you. Are there degrees of your kind of love as well as different kinds?'

'Lynn, my dear, I'm not exactly an authority on the subject! You can hardly call me experienced, can you? But from watching people's marriages . . . from my own inner convictions, I have learned that there is always one partner who cares just a little bit more than the other. I don't know why it should be. I have often thought that it is because, human nature being what it is, one perversely puts a greater value on that which is more difficult to obtain. In the beginning of a friendship, one person becomes aware before the other that they are "in love". That starts the chase, does it not? For a time, however short, one will be afraid that the other does not love, might not care. So success, when it comes, is valued a little more by him or her than by the one who wakes up to find love waiting.'

Lynn smiled, a quiet, lovely smile which touched his heart just as her words brought the greatest moment of happiness to him.

'Pip, I will marry you . . . if only because you always have the right answer for all the things which puzzle me. I have "woken up to find love waiting" and it is a warm, glorious happy feeling. I'll try not to take advantage of it.'

'My dearest one, you could not . . . even if you tried.'

He took her hand and held it firmly between his own as they smiled into each other's eyes.

*   *   *

It was January, a year later. The wedding lunch was over and it was nearly time for Lynn to join her husband who was waiting downstairs for her with Jack. Marion, noticing Lynn's deliberate attempts to conceal the pallor of her cheekbones with rouge, looked at her anxiously.

'No regrets, darling?'

Lynn carefully wet her forefinger and smoothed her eyebrows.

'No,' she said slowly, and Marion could not be sure if there had been any hesitation in the reply or not.

It had been a quiet wedding in the registrar's office near Marion's flat. Jack, of course, had been best man and Marion matron of honour. Lynn's aunt had brought David and Sue, although right up to the last hour Lynn had not been sure if she would permit them to be there, saying over and over again to Marion:

'But I'm not sure it would be *right*, Marion. I want them to accept Philip in their own time. They're too young to understand properly.'

'Then why not let them be there since they are so eager to go!' Marion had replied for the umpteenth time. 'They don't want to be left out of what they see as a party! What does Philip say about it?'

Lynn had smiled briefly.

'That I must do exactly as I wish. If only I knew what was best, Marion!'

It seemed strange to Marion that since the moment Lynn had decided to marry Philip and had told them all that she was going to do so, all certainty had left her. Even over the choice of wedding attire, time of day for the ceremony or where they might honeymoon, Lynn was hopelessly undecided, vacillating

252

first one way then another.

'You're quite sure you *want* to marry Pip?' Marion had asked her more than once.

'But of course!' Lynn had replied, her eyes surprised as if she were not aware of the change in herself since their engagement. She seemed unaware of the soberness of her expression and the lack of outward happiness that usually haloed a happy woman soon to marry the man of her choice.

Pip looked worried, too. And, consequently, devoted as she was to them both, Marion had felt her own pleasure in what to her was the perfect solution to the problem of Lynn's life, giving way to doubts.

'I expect it's just pre-wedding nerves!' Jack comforted her in his usual placid fashion.

'If only I could be sure Lynn is not still a bit in love with Jerry! She swears it isn't so; that the last time she saw him when he came to say good-bye, she knew finally it was all over; that there wasn't a spark of feeling left for him. It's not so much that, I think, as the fact that she may not be really in love with Pip. He does so worship her, Jack. It would be perfectly awful for them both if this went wrong.'

'They'll be all right,' was Jack's comment, 'and even if they aren't, there isn't a thing you can or should do about them at this stage.'

The weeks before the wedding had crept by on leaden feet . . . or so Marion thought. Lynn spent a great deal of her time shopping for her trousseau. 'I must have everything quite new, Marion . . . nothing at all to remind me of the past.' This, like practically every similar comment Lynn made only increased Marion's concern for her brother-in-law and her dearest friend.

Now it was all over . . . for better or for worse, and Lynn would be departing on her honeymoon within a matter of minutes. It had been silly of her to ask Lynn if she regretted what she had just done with her life, her future. It was too late now to regret it. If only she could be sure Lynn was going to be happy!

'Lynn, darling, I do wish with all my heart that you and Pip will be happy together!'

Lynn smiled a curiously wistful smile as she turned from the mirror to face Marion.

'That's sweet of you, Marion. And I'm so terribly grateful for everything you have done. It . . .' her voice faltered . . . 'it wasn't a very easy or happy time and you've been a rock of strength and comfort. I'm so happy to have you as a friend.'

Impulsively, Marion flung her arms round Lynn's shoulders in an unusual outward demonstration of affection, and kissed her on the carefully rouged cheek.

Suddenly tears sprang into Lynn's eyes and as Marion stared at her aghast, Lynn made a great effort and controlled the threatening sobs that were in her throat.

'I . . . I wish I had time for a nice cup of tea!'

she whispered, smiling through the brief tears that she had been unable to control.

Marion pushed her back into the chair and said firmly: 'Then you shall have a cup of tea, Poppet. Just wait while I fix it.'

'No, I didn't really mean it!' Lynn said, wiping her eyes and touching up the powder on her face. 'Really, Marion . . . look, the truth is . . . I'm scared.'

Marion gave a laugh of pure relief.

'Lynn, you idiot! It never occurred to me you'd have honeymoon nerves. I thought something else was wrong; that you might be sorry you'd married Pip or something ghastly like that!'

'Well, in a way, that's what I'm scared about,' Lynn said in a quiet trembling voice. Now that she had confided a little of her emotions to Marion, it seemed as if she could not stop the rush of confidences. 'You see, I'm so terribly afraid I'll fail him. Marion, you can't begin to know how wonderful he has been. He seems to sense my feelings, and by some queer inner instinct he has always fitted his mood so perfectly to mine that there has never been a jarring note.'

'Then surely you have no need to worry now? Pip can be that way with you because he loves you. Loving gives you that instinct. Nothing can go wrong.'

Lynn looked at Marion from wide eyes.

'But don't you see, we can't go on like that.

Philip has been terribly patient; he has done all the giving and none of the taking. If our marriage is going to work, I must give him something, too.'

'But you do love him, Lynn?'

'Of course, *of course* I do! I would never have married him if I hadn't loved him. Surely you know that. But it is dispassionate love, Marion. During these weeks of our engagement, we never made love. I think Philip guessed that I didn't want that kind of love from him.'

'But surely he has kissed you?' Marion exclaimed. For a brief moment, Lynn laughed naturally.

'Yes, of course he has, Marion. But there are kisses and kisses, aren't there? Philip and I have behaved rather as if we were very dear friends. But we are married now, Marion, and we can't go on like that. I suppose I could . . . that's what I really want, but I *know* Philip couldn't. Nor do I expect he should. That's why I'm scared. Suppose I can't respond physically the way I did with Jerry!'

Marion remained silent. This was an aspect of Lynn's relationship with Philip that had never crossed her mind. It had simply not occurred to her. Yet surely it should have done! She had realized at the end of Lynn's marriage to Jerry that it had been based all along on a strong physical passion; that both Lynn and Jerry were highly emotional, passionate people. No doubt the perfection of that side of their marriage was what had kept it alive for so long. Now Lynn was afraid that she must fail Philip because she didn't feel the same physical attraction that she had once felt for Jerry. Poor girl!

'Lynn, I don't think you ought to think about it; I believe this is something you should let happen naturally without too much consideration beforehand.'

'I suspect that you are right!' Lynn said with a wry smile. 'But the suggestion comes a little late. I've thought of little else ever since I promised to marry Philip. I love him, Marion, I really do. I think I love him far more sincerely, deeply, than I ever loved Jerry. But the truth is, Jerry and I were perfectly matched. We were absolutely in tune sexually. Everything else could . . . and did . . . go wrong with our marriage, but never that. I got used to him, Marion. So many years of married life can do that to you. Now I'm marrying because I love with my mind, not with my body. That's what is so dreadful. I'm physically dead.'

'It is the emotional strain . . . nothing more!' Marion said with a confidence she was far from feeling. 'Maybe you should have seen a psychologist, Lynn! Oh, darling, I wish you'd talked to me about it before. I'll be so worried about you.'

Lynn stood up and she was calm again, and quite in control of her emotions.

'Don't worry, Marion. I expect it will work itself out. And thank you again for everything. It's comforting to know that our friendship is now doubly tied with the extra tag of "sister-in-law". And I shall always thank you for having introduced me to Philip. I'll try to make him happy!'

This was the reason why Philip's brother, Jack, found his wife crying later that evening. He put his arms round her and told her gently not to be such a silly goose.

'Pip's no fool!' he said. 'He'll understand. He won't rush her!'

'But Jack, he doesn't know the first thing about women. You're asking him to understand some twisted part in Lynn that no man could understand without being told, and I know she hasn't told him.'

'There's such a thing as a man's intuition, although I'm fully aware that you women like to imagine you have the sole right to that,' Jack said, as he took her in his arms. 'Dash it all, old thing, I didn't know much about women when I married you, and I didn't do so badly on our honeymoon, did I?'

'Oh, darling!' Marion whispered as she snuggled against his shoulder. 'I'm so glad you married me! I just hope Lynn and Pip will be as happy as we are.'

* * *

Lynn's nervous tension eased a little on the train ride from Victoria to Dover. She even began to feel excited at the thought of two whole weeks in a luxurious hotel in Paris. She and Philip were both good sailors and, whatever the weather, would enjoy the Channel crossing. In the train, he sat opposite her and, perhaps because of the other people in the carriage, refrained from making any remarks of a personal nature. Confetti had hardly been in keeping with the quiet wedding they had preferred and there was nothing to indicate that they were newlyweds setting out on a honeymoon. In fact, Lynn thought, glancing across her glossy magazine at Philip reading the late night stock-market prices in his evening paper, they might have been no more than casual friends; or else have been married for so long that they had no more to say to one another! She felt a smile come to her lips and, glancing up at that moment, Philip met her eyes and smiled back. It was a moment of complete intimacy, isolating them from the strangers on either side of them and drawing them very close.

It'll be all right! Lynn thought.

This feeling of reassurance lasted until they reached the hotel. Then suddenly nerves reassailed her. She tried to tell herself she was tired, but she knew that in truth she had begun to do the very thing she most dreaded . . . remember that other honeymoon; that first wonderful, perfect moment of her life when she had heard Jerry say, 'A double room booked for Mr. and Mrs. Gerald Birch!' Now she could hear Philip's voice saying, 'Mr. and Mrs. Philip Castle!'

That isn't me . . . it isn't me! she thought wildly, as Philip signed the register.

Their bedroom, vast as it was, was filled with flowers. Seeing first the twin beds, then the masses of palest yellow rosebuds on the bed-table, Lynn knew the first moment of relief. It wasn't the same. Jerry had not thought of flowers . . . only a bottle of champagne.

'You are pleased, Madame? The flowers Monsieur order are very beautiful, *non*?'

'They are beautiful,' Lynn told the hotel manager who, she correctly surmised, must have been very well tipped indeed by Philip to be showing them to their room in person. She knew that they would lack nothing at all for their comfort while they were here. Philip was determined that everything should be quite perfect. Then nerves caused her to draw in her breath and turn her face quickly away. It was always Philip who was giving. Could she give him something, too? Or would her offering be empty; void of the response he must want from her?

The door closed behind the hotel manager and they were suddenly alone. Lynn said:

'I'll unpack, I think. My clothes will be so squashed if I leave them till morning.'

260

She heard Philip moving across the room behind her.

'I shouldn't do more than you feel necessary, Lynn. It's pretty late and you must be tired out. Anything you'd like me to order for you . . . a drink, tea?'

'I would love a cup of tea . . . no, coffee!' Lynn said.

'I thought I'd go down to the bar for a nightcap,' she heard Philip's voice; 'that is, if you don't mind my going, darling. I'll order your coffee as I go down.'

'I'd come with you but I *am* tired,' Lynn admitted, knowing that her real reason for refusal was her wish to be alone. But after Philip had gone, she felt perversely lonely. The room, centrally heated, bathed in a warm glow from the concealed lighting, perfumed by the masses of roses, was suddenly alien. She started to think about the children . . . missing them, needing them.

She wanted to be able to go along a passage and open David's door; see his face rosy with sleep, his mouth pouting, his hands stretched out above the covers. She wanted to see Sue sleeping as she always did on her tummy, her legs bunched up beneath her so that David nicknamed her 'the camel'! They were unbearably far away and the all-too-ready tears stung and pricked her eyelids as she slowly unsnapped the lock of the first suitcase.

I mustn't cry . . . *I mustn't!* she thought

hysterically. Pip may come back any moment. I won't unpack. I'll have a hot bath and then get into bed and leave the unpacking until tomorrow.

She was in bed sipping the hot, delicious French coffee when finally Pip returned to their room. He came in and seeing her, smiled contentedly.

'I'm sure that's the best place to be!' he said. 'I'm dog-tired, too. You look very lovely, Lynn . . . but then you always do.'

He sat down quite naturally on the edge of her bed and took her hand . . . the hand that now held his wedding ring.

'There were an odd lot of blokes in the bar!' he said for no reason at all. 'I enjoyed the drink, but I missed you!'

'Philip, thank you for everything. I . . . I love you very much!'

He looked down at his ring, twisting it a little round her finger.

'You've made me so happy, darling!' he said after a pause. 'I never dared dream that this could happen; that my dream would come true!'

She knew he was thinking back to the first time he had met her; the moment he had fallen in love with her, he had since told her. Not that he had known it then. Realization had not come till later. But by a tacit understanding, neither spoke much of the past. The past held Jerry, and a wealth of

262

unhappiness accompanied those memories. Now she was Philip's wife and she knew that soon he might start to regret his marriage. She felt her muscles stiffen and was afraid that he would notice the sudden cold chill of her hand. She drew it casually away from his grasp, saying:

'It's a real Hollywood bathroom, Philip . . . all green and silver.'

He got up from the bed and she noticed inconsequently how tall he was; how shaggy and bearlike . . . not the least little bit in keeping with the smart sophistication of the bedroom. A wave of tenderness swept through her and then fear returned. She lay back on the pillows, her hands clenched, waiting.

Tiredness forced her eyes shut but she was not sleeping when Philip came out of the bathroom and climbed into the bed beside hers. She fought against the desire to feign sleep because it was cowardly and proved nothing, and opening her eyes, she looked across at him. He was yawning and stretching his arms above his head.

'God, I'm tired!' he said, yawning again. 'Shall I put out the light, Lynn? You look so young lying on the pillow. I shall be put in quod for baby-snatching!'

Without waiting for her reply, he switched off the reading lamps above their beds and she heard him yawn again.

The silence, broken only by their breathing,

became quite intolerable to Lynn. She had wanted the darkness and now she wanted the security of light. Presently she said into the darkness:

'Are you asleep, Phil?'

'Almost!' his voice came back at her.

Silence fell again, and Lynn controlled the trembling of her body sufficiently to trust her voice again. Surely Philip did not intend to leave this situation unresolved. Then she realized that for him there probably was no question to be answered. He could know nothing of her physical reluctance; of her fear, her qualms. He was simply behaving naturally. Could he possibly be so tired that he was prepared to leave the first night of their honeymoon like this . . . the two of them sleeping in twin beds, side by side, as if they had been married for years, not hours?

'Philip?'

'Uh-huh?'

'Talk to me a little bit. I'm tired but I can't sleep. So much has happened today and . . .' Her voice broke suddenly and, try as she might, she could not continue. Again she felt tears pricking her eyelids and she hated herself. She stifled her face against the pillow, hearing only the muffled tones of Philip's deep voice. Then suddenly the sense of his words began to penetrate her mind and she sat up in the darkness, her hands clutching the sheets.

'. . . I've known you didn't want anything

264

more from our marriage than friendship, companionship, and I'm prepared to leave it that way. Never, never feel that you must do anything that you don't wish to do, Lynn. I'm happy with my share of the bargain and all I want in return is that you should be happy with yours. Whatever happens, darling, please don't be afraid of me. I know you've tried to hide it; but that fear is there and it hurts terribly to know it . . .'

'Oh, Philip!' She was scrambling across the brief space between their beds, searching in the darkness for him, her hands finding his face and holding it tenderly as she whispered his name. She was shivering and a moment later she was lying against the welcome warmth of his body. She was no longer afraid. In a few words he had banished her fear and she knew through her tenderness and love for this man who was so good to her that something else had been born. She needed him; needed his desire for her as a woman. The fierce natural fires of her body had been rekindled by the pure flame of love for him that filled her whole being.

As his arms went round her, she felt no fear or tension but a perfect, wonderful emotion of happiness. She was safe; safe in love; safe to give all herself and her love; safe in the knowledge that she would never be betrayed again.

'Philip, dearest, darling Pip!' she murmured.

265

'This is where my heart is!' and she placed her soft warm fingers against his own fiercely beating heart.

*   *   *

David to Lynn

Dear Mum,
I hoap you are having a nice hollyday. I am conting the days till Wensday. Sue and me is very incited abart living at the Manner House. Uncle Pip sed at the wedding we cud have a pony next holls. Aunty Marion took us to the Curcuss. It was great.
Love from David.
P.S. Sue sends a kiss.

January. Mary to Mrs. Philip Castle.

Dear Mrs. Castle,
I am writing like I said to tell you the children are all well and looking forward to your return. Mrs. Jack says I am to go down to the Manor House before you come home to get everything ready and she'll drive the children down Wednesday morning. This seems very satisfactory. Baby Paul was trying hard to walk this morning. I dare say he's only waiting to show off in front of you.
I hope this finds you as it leaves me, which is in good health.

266

Yours faithfully,
Mary.
P.S. I forwarded some letters yesterday. I hope they arrive at the hotel.

January. Matron of St. Stephen's Home to Mr. and Mrs. Philip Castle.

Dear Mr. and Mrs. Castle,
I am glad to tell you that I spoke to the Children's Officer today about Baby Stephanie and there is no reason why Baby should not come to you as soon as you return from your holiday. There was a satisfactory report from the Children's Officer in Kent about the home Baby will have and I think it would be quite fair to say that your adoption of Baby will be through in three or four months time. According to your request, the mother is not being told who is having the baby but has written again to us stating her willingness to leave the matter in my hands.
May I take this opportunity of wishing you both every possible happiness in your new life together, a happiness I am sure you both deserve. May God bless you both as I am sure He will do!
Yours very sincerely,
Elizabeth Harrow.

May. Lynn to Marion.

My dearest sister-in-law!

I have been meaning to write to you for days but we have been so excited by the Court order making Stephanie ours that I haven't known whether I was on my head or my heels. All the local people think she's Paul's twin and the likeness that so astounded you last time you saw her is even more pronounced now.

Oh, Marion, I am so happy . . . so perfectly and wonderfully happy, I hardly dare breathe for spoiling any tiny particle of this perfection. It's so glorious here for one thing. Do you realize that it is two years since that day you, Jack, Philip and the children and I came here on a picnic and I saw Manor House for the first time? It seems another world and I walk round my home and garden with a feeling that I've always lived in and loved this place; that it is my spiritual home.

Philip is the perfect husband. I know I don't deserve the way he spoils me. And the children just adore him. Of his own accord the other day David suddenly called him 'Dad'. Philip was thrilled although he didn't show it much. Sue always copies David so it won't be long before she does the same. I think she has practically forgotten her father, anyway. And David never seemed to miss him or mind his going away when he did. As for Paul and Stephanie . . . well, they won't ever remember Jerry. It's strange how I can think of him now without hatred or bitterness. I am reminded of him from time to time but his name means nothing to me now. I'm far too happy in my new life to be able to bear anyone a grudge, far less the man who indirectly threw my into Philip's arms.

Come and see us soon. You and Jack are our most popular visitors as you both know full well. Besides, I think I may have some news for you both which, if it is true, will be the last drop of happiness either Philip or I could draw from life. How would you and Jack like a real live nephew or niece? Oh, my dear, don't tell me we have enough kids as it is. Philip has set his heart on one more to make up the five. It's as if he has been able to recapture his childhood once again.

Mary is taking Paul and Stephanie for a walk and will post this for me so I'll finish now by sending you lots of love.

Your contented and gloriously happy,
Lynn.

May. Jerry to Lynn.

Dear Lynn,

I read in an old copy of The Times *I happened to find the other day that you had married again. I must admit that I felt a bit hurt that you had not informed me about it earlier though I have since had, of course, a letter from your solicitor via mine saying that you wished to discontinue accepting an allowance from me for the children. I suppose I can understand your reasons for this although I feel I have a right, as their father, to pay for them if I wish.*

Don't worry! I won't start an argument on the subject. I know I treated you pretty shabbily and I'm willing to take a back seat now in so far as the children are concerned. It seems even more improbable that I shall get back to England for some years yet so you won't have the problem of sharing them with me . . . reasonable access, didn't the judge call it?

I suppose I should wish you every happiness in your new marriage. I do. I think you deserve it. All the same, I can't help being surprised at your choice. Not that I'm saying anything against Castle. I hardly knew him, but I suspect that he is the same reliable, stolid type as Jack. Maybe this is why you picked him! At least you will be able to count on him whereas you were never too sure of me, were you? You may not believe it, but during the whole of our marriage I never actually loved any other woman . . . only made love to them, but I suppose that's just as much a sin in your eyes.

As for myself if you should be interested, I married six months ago and am living in New York. To be truthful, I can't say I am too happy with my choice although I had a reasonably good idea what I was doing as I think I told you. I certainly don't need to worry about money. Nevertheless, American women expect their husbands to behave like slaves or lap dogs, and my wife is constantly pulling me up for my shortcomings in this respect. You never nagged. It does so spoil a woman. I suppose it is only right that I should earn my share in the luxuries of this world but I was mistaken in believing that my work would be confined to the office. I wonder if you will derive any satisfaction from my no doubt obvious discontent? I imagine not, since you were never vindictive. You see, my dear, I can and always did appreciate your good qualities but unfortunately could not myself live up to them.

Remember me sometimes, Lynn . . . that is if you can do so kindly. I leave it to you to give my love to David and Sue if you choose. Maybe you prefer them to forget me, and perhaps, after all, that is best. The past is past and there is no going back. Come to that, I think it would be for the best if I did not come back to England. I should certainly not enjoy haunting memories of our life together knowing that it can never be reincarnated.

I'm damned sorry, Lynn, that I failed. I do genuinely hope you will find happiness now and by doing so, can be lenient in your thoughts towards me . . . if any. I shan't write in this vein again. I just wanted you to know that I regret my shortcomings quite as much as you must have done and I truly believe, as you must, that you are well rid of me.

Au revoir, my dear ... or as I think it really is this time, good-bye. Somehow I feel we are not likely to cross paths again but I shan't forget you.

Jerry.

Lynn leant forward in her chair and quietly placed the letter in the fire. She watched it twist and turn in a bright flame, then crumble and disappear among the embers. For a moment longer she stared at the ashes; then raising her head to find Philip's eyes on her, she relaxed and gave him her warm, loving smile.